KU-024-246

ONE

The trouble with tropical paradises, thought Keith as he sprinted out of the school building, is that everyone's too relaxed.

He swerved to avoid a year four kid strolling along sucking a mango, leapt over a group of year three's sprawled under the palm trees swapping shells, and glanced at his watch.

Sixteen minutes past three.

Only two hours and forty-nine minutes left.

Thanks a lot Mr Gerlach, thought Keith bitterly. There ought to be a law against teachers being that relaxed. Yakking on for thirteen minutes after the bell. Couldn't he see when a person's guts were in knots because a person was running out of time?

Keith hurtled out of the school gate, skidded to avoid a year five kid trying to crack a coconut with a recorder, and sprinted along the dusty street towards the shops. He glanced at his watch again.

Two hours and forty-eight minutes left.

Would it be enough?

He felt the knot tightening in his guts.

Calm down, he thought. I'll be OK as long as Mrs Newman in the post office doesn't start yakking on about her grandson.

I

Mrs Newman in the post office started yakking on about her grandson.

'Only seventeen months old,' she said to Keith, 'and he can say prawn.'

Pick up the savings book, thought Keith. Pick it up.

Mrs Newman picked up Keith's savings book from the counter.

'Gee,' she said, looking at the withdrawal slip, 'thirty-eight dollars. Are you sure you want to take all that out in one go?'

No, thought Keith, I want a one cent coin every Friday for the next fourteen thousand years.

'Yes,' said Keith. 'And I'm in a bit of a hurry thanks.'

He glanced up at the post office clock.

Two hours and forty-one minutes left.

'That only leaves one dollar and twenty-seven cents in your account,' said Mrs Newman.

'That's right,' said Keith.

'Must be for something important, thirty-eight dollars,' said Mrs Newman.

'It is,' said Keith.

'That's good,' she said, 'cause it'd be a shame to take out thirty-eight dollars and just fritter it away.'

'Mrs Newman,' said Keith, 'I had to peel seven hundred and sixty potatoes to earn that money. I'm not going to fritter away seven hundred and sixty potatoes.'

Mrs Newman smiled and started writing slowly in his savings book.

2

Keith looked up at the clock again. Two hours and forty minutes left.

Mrs Newman stopped writing.

Oh no, thought Keith. Please don't ask me how I'm liking Australia. Not again. I haven't got time.

'How are you liking Australia?' asked Mrs Newman.

'Fine thanks,' said Keith, making a mental note to write to the council and ask when Orchid Cove would be getting an automatic bank machine.

Mrs Newman wrote a couple more numbers, then stopped and looked up again. 'Tell your mum and dad I'm sorry I couldn't get in for my fish and chips yesterday, but Gail had to get her feet done and I had Shaun and Alex so we had baked beans. How are your mum's feet?'

'Fine thanks,' said Keith, sighing.

'The trouble with North Queensland,' said Mrs Newman, 'is that your feet swell up.'

The trouble with North Queensland, thought Keith, is that everyone's too friendly.

He glanced at his watch.

Two hours and thirty-nine minutes left.

No need to panic, he thought. I'll be OK as long as there's not a queue in the hardware store.

Keith stood in the queue in the hardware store and started to panic.

Two hours and thirty-two minutes left.

He was running out of time.

Relax, he told himself. It's only a short queue, just Gary Murdoch and his dad. They can't need that much hardware cause they only moved into their new house three weeks ago.

'Tap washers,' said Mr Murdoch to the assistant. 'You wouldn't credit it. Brand new place, all the taps are dripping.'

Keith's heart sank. Gary had been boasting all week in class about how his new house had twenty-seven taps. This could take ages.

'How many?' asked the assistant.

Mr Murdoch started counting in his head.

'Twenty-seven,' said Keith.

Gary and Mr Murdoch both turned round.

'G'day Keith,' said Gary. 'Dad, this is Keith Shipley, the kid I was telling you about.'

'G'day,' said Mr Murdoch, looking down at Keith with a grin. 'You're the bloke dragged his parents out here from pommyland to cheer 'em up, right?'

'I didn't drag them,' said Keith, 'they agreed to come.'

'Only after you burnt half the street down, but, eh?' said Gary.

'It was just one fish and chip shop and it was an accident,' said Keith, hoping the dripping tap in Gary Murdoch's ensuite bathroom flooded his bedroom and made his Walkman go rusty.

'Has it worked?' asked Mr Murdoch. 'Have they cheered up?'

'Actually,' said Keith, 'if you don't mind I'm in a bit of a hurry.'

'There,' said the assistant, scooping a pile of washers into a bag, 'twenty-seven.'

4

Mr Murdoch ignored him. He looked hard at Keith. 'Bowls,' he said. 'Get 'em to join the bowls club, that'll cheer 'em up. And if they're having a house built, tell 'em to watch the taps.'

The trouble with tropical paradises, thought Keith, glancing at his watch, is that everyone's too helpful.

Keith sprinted out of the hardware store, paint cans thumping together in his school bag.

The clock on the war memorial across the street said eight minutes past eleven. Keith stared. Then he remembered it had been wrong ever since a coconut had hit it in the cyclone.

He looked at his watch. Nineteen minutes to four. Two hours and twenty-four minutes left.

He should just make it.

As long as Mum and Dad didn't see him.

Keith decided he'd better not risk going too close to the shop so he ran across the road, through the fringe of palm trees and on to the beach. He ran along the soft sand, trying to look like a tourist out for a jog with a couple of tins of paint in his school bag.

He glanced through the palm trees at the shop.

Mum and Dad were both behind the counter but neither of them was looking in his direction. They were looking at each other. Dad was saying something to Mum, pointing at her with a piece of fish, and Mum was saying something back, waving the chip scoop at him.

Even at that distance, Keith could see that Dad's mouth was droopier than a palm frond and that

Mum's forehead had more furrows in it than wet sand when the sea was a bit choppy.

Keith's stomach knotted even tighter.

Another argument.

Poor things. Stuck in a fish and chip shop all day in this heat. Anyone'd get a bit irritable standing over a fryer all day with this poxy sun pounding down non-stop.

The trouble with tropical paradises, thought Keith as he ran on along the beach, is that there's too much good weather.

He went back up to the road and crossed it at the spot where the bus from the airport had dropped them four months earlier.

He remembered Mum and Dad's faces, aglow with huge smiles as they saw Orchid Cove for the first time.

All they need is a bit of cheering up again, thought Keith as he sprinted towards the house. Which is exactly what they'll get when they arrive home in two hours and twenty-one minutes.

TWO

Keith looked at his watch. Forty-seven minutes left and he'd almost finished.

Not bad going, he thought, considering it's the first time I've ever painted a car.

He crouched down to do a bit he'd missed at the bottom of a wheel arch, and noticed that one of the back tyres was a bit flat.

Stands to reason, he thought. Sitting out here in front of the house for weeks without being driven.

While he did around the number plate he tried to remember the last Sunday they'd gone for a drive. Was it the time they went down to Mission Beach and Dad dropped his ice-cream and they all had a good laugh and then Mum got a migraine? Or was it the day they went to the crocodile farm and Mum insisted on having lunch in the café there and Dad got the trots?

Keith couldn't remember.

Anyway, he thought, as he finished off the exhaust pipe, it was before Mum took up Sunday bush walking and Dad took up Sunday crosswords. Which hadn't fooled Keith for a moment. He knew exactly why Mum and Dad didn't want to go out for Sunday drives anymore.

They were embarrassed.

Embarrassed to be seen driving around in an off-white 1979 Toyota Corolla with rust spots when Gary Murdoch's dad had a bright-red 1990 Mercedes with speed stripes and chrome wheels.

Well you won't have to be embarrassed anymore, thought Keith.

He put a second coat on the dent Mum had made in the passenger door the day she flung it open and hit a steel girder.

Keith shuddered as he remembered that day.

They'd been parked in the drive-in bottle shop. Mum and Dad had been arguing about which beer to buy.

The trouble with tropical paradises, thought Keith as he put a third coat on the dent, is that there are too many brands of beer.

'Jeez.'

Keith turned at the sound of the familiar voice.

Tracy stood there looking at the car.

'It's a bit bright, but,' she said.

That's a good one, thought Keith, coming from a girl with a luminous orange and purple skateboard. And pink patches on her face where the brown was peeling off.

'It's a wedding anniversary present for my mum and dad,' he said.

'Hope you got them sunglasses as well,' said Tracy.

A twinge of panic hit Keith under the ribs. Perhaps it was a bit bright. The Tropical Mango he'd painted

the shop in England with had been a bit bright and they hadn't liked that at first.

Relax, he told himself, this is different. Mum and Dad were misery guts then. Now they're cheerful, adventurous globe-trotters who are just feeling the heat a bit. Don't be a worry wart.

The panic went as he remembered how Dad had stared enviously the first time Mr Murdoch had driven past in his bright-red Mercedes.

'Do they know about it?' asked Tracy.

'It's a surprise,' he said.

'It'll be a surprise all right,' said Tracy, 'when they find they've got the only green car with yellow stripes in the whole of Far North Queensland.'

'It's not green and yellow,' said Keith, 'it's Tropical Parrot and Hot Sunflower. And they're speed stripes.'

'Gary Murdoch's dad'll chuck his guts with envy when he sees that,' said Tracy, grinning at him.

Keith grinned back. Good old Tracy. You could trust a mate to say the right thing.

'What made you choose green and yellow?' asked Tracy.

'I wanted it to be Mum and Dad's favourite colours,' said Keith, 'so I checked out their wardrobe. Mum's got three separate things that are green and yellow stripes and Dad's got a yellow shirt and green socks.'

'Jeez, you're a clever mongrel,' said Tracy.

Keith glowed. When some kids said that they were sending you up, but when Tracy said it you knew she meant it.

'Is this why you nicked off after school without hanging around for softball?' she asked.

'Sorry,' said Keith, 'I was on a tight deadline. I only had the idea in art. Had to make sure I got it finished before Mum and Dad got home from the shop.'

'They don't get home for another forty minutes,' said Tracy.

'Thirty-nine,' said Keith, 'thirty-eight if they walk fast.'

'Jeez, you're a worry wart,' said Tracy, grinning at him again.

He asked her whether she thought he should do the bumper bars to disguise the dent where Dad had backed into a concrete post in the Cairns car-park the day Mum had bought her green and yellow striped swimming costume.

Tracy said she reckoned he should leave them in case his mum bought some more expensive clothes and his dad backed into something else, which would only chip the paint.

Keith agreed.

'Gotta go now,' said Tracy, 'gotta help clean out the chooks. See you down the beach later?'

'Maybe,' said Keith.

He didn't want to be more definite because there was always the chance that when Mum and Dad saw the paint job they'd want Keith to leap straight into the car with them and drive up to Port Douglas to have a pizza in the outdoor restaurant under the fairy lights, where they'd all clink their glasses together, or their metal containers if they were having milkshakes, and toast their happiness together for ever and ever.

One minute to go.

Keith did a final check. Camera. Anniversary card. Ribbon.

He hoped Mum and Dad wouldn't mind about the ribbon. He hadn't been able to find one long enough to go round a car. The clothes-line looked OK anyway, even if the bow was a bit floppy.

The anniversary card looked great, standing on the bonnet. Now it was painted you couldn't see it was made from bits of Chicko Roll boxes. The Hot Sunflower *Happy Wedding Anniversary* stood out really well against the Tropical Parrot.

He checked round the car for drips.

Hardly any.

It had really paid off, using quick-drying plastic paint. Much better than the gloss stuff he'd used on the shop in England, which had taken a week to dry just because there'd been a bit of rain.

Keith glanced at his watch.

Six minutes past six.

Where were they?

Perhaps they were still at the shop arguing and they hadn't noticed the time.

Keith tried to force that awful thought out of his mind.

He still hadn't managed to when Mum and Dad came round the corner.

Keith took a deep breath.

'Happy wedding anniversary,' he shouted, squinting into the camera.

He wanted to get their faces the moment they broke into huge glowing grins.

Through the viewfinder he could see them moving towards him, eyes wide and mouths open.

Come on, thought Keith, let's have the delighted smiles.

'Happy wedding anniversary,' he shouted again.

Mum and Dad were very close now, eyes still wide and mouths still open.

Come on, thought Keith, smile or you'll be out of focus.

He pressed the button anyway, just as Mum started to cry.

After Dad had taken Mum into the house, Keith stared at the car for a long while, trying to think.

Why hadn't they said anything about the paint job?

Because they hadn't needed to, probably. Tears from Mum and a mouth drooping almost to the ground from Dad had said it all.

They didn't like it.

Keith felt his eyes getting hot.

Pull yourself together, he thought. Be positive. Why don't they like it?

The colours?

The unpainted bumper bars?

The fact that I only put one 'n' in 'anniversary'?

No problem, he said to himself.

If they're worried about my spelling I'll do extra homework.

If they're upset about the bumper bars I'll paint them.

If they don't like Tropical Parrot and Hot Sunflower I'll have the whole car another colour by tomorrow night. Off-white if they want.

Suddenly he felt much better.

Trust Mum and Dad to make a big drama out of such a simple problem, whichever one it was.

Keith went into the house, working out how many kids he'd have to borrow a dollar from to buy two litres of off-white paint.

Mum and Dad were in their bedroom, talking.

Keith didn't mean to listen, but their voices came clearly through the thin wall.

'We can't carry on like this,' said Mum's voice tearfully.

'What about Keith?' said Dad's voice.

Keith was shocked. Dad's voice sounded like he'd been crying too.

'Plenty of kids' parents split up,' said Mum's shaking voice, 'it's not the end of the world.'

Keith stood in the narrow, hot hallway and the blood pounded in his ears so loudly that he thought for a few seconds another cyclone had hit.

Then he ran out of the house.

THREE

Keith didn't stop running till he got to the beach. He threw himself down on the sand under a palm tree and squeezed his eyes shut.

He wished he could open them and find himself back in England, even somewhere boring like Watford or Lancashire, just so long as things were back to normal and there was a fish and chip shop with Mum and Dad in it, with only slightly miserable faces, together, as usual.

Or France. Or Russia.

Anywhere, he thought bitterly, except this poxy so-called tropical paradise.

He stared up at the sunset. The sky was rippled with pink and orange and purple. It looked like the time Ryan Garner pinched nine packets of lollies and threw up on the monkey bars.

The darkening air was loud with the screech of insects. Cicadas being negative. Mosquitoes being defeatist. Grasshoppers lying to their kids about the state of their marriage.

Keith felt hot tears.

'Shut up,' he shouted at the grasshoppers.

He took a deep breath. The tropical evening smells made him feel sick. He could smell rotting fruit and squashed cane toads and poisonous flowers that paralysed their victims with squirts of rancid liquid. Probably their kids too.

For the hundredth time since running out of the house he tried to think of something else that Mum could have been saying.

Something other than split up.

He couldn't.

He stared at the ocean. The waves were pink and frothy and looked like toothpaste that had been spat out by someone with a bleeding gum.

He thought about what was probably going on under the water. Stonefish not talking to each other. Pufferfish having arguments and getting migraines. Killer jellyfish splitting up and emotionally neglecting their kids.

The hot tears wouldn't stop.

I wish, thought Keith, I'd never brought Mum and Dad to this poxy, stinking, rat-hole of a dump.

They were OK in England. Misery guts, yes, but a holiday would have fixed that.

Wait a sec.

A holiday.

Suddenly his mind was racing.

He tried to remember the last time Mum and Dad had been on holiday.

Five years ago?

Ten?

Being in this dump didn't count. All they were doing here was what they used to do in England, slaving over a fryer and a bowl of batter, and being miserable.

Except here it was worse because they were in a poxy, overheated, so-called tropical paradise.

No wonder they were getting irritable and stressed and imagining they didn't want to be together any more.

A holiday, that's what they needed.

Keith scrambled to his feet, tears gone, heart pounding with excitement.

He needed some holiday details fast and he knew just where to get them.

'There you go,' said Tracy, 'take your pick.'

She dropped the last bundle of brochures on to her bed.

Keith stared.

There were thousands.

He'd seen bits of Tracy's travel brochure collection before, but never the whole lot at once.

'OK,' said Tracy, 'this bundle is adventure holidays, this one is mountain ranges, this is old cities, this is modern cities, this is campsites with views, this is campsites without views, this is relics of ancient civilizations, this is cruises, this is traditional villages in remote valleys untouched by the modern world, this is places that are flat but interesting, and this is tropical paradises, except you probably won't want that one.'

Dead right, thought Keith as he dropped to his knees and grabbed the first bundle.

A thought hit him. Probably better to stick to this end of the world. That way Mum and Dad won't feel they've wasted their money coming all the way down here.

He told Tracy this and she explained that the Australia and New Zealand brochures were at the back of each bundle.

He started pulling out brochures.

'You're sure she said split up?' asked Tracy, kneeling down next to him. 'Mr Gambaso in the milk bar sold my dad a hamburger once with a bit of bone in it and Dad broke a filling and said he'd kill him. I was on the roof chasing cane toads and I freaked and hid his fish-gutting knife. Turned out he'd said he'd bill him.'

'Mum said it,' replied Keith, 'but she didn't mean it. She's under stress.'

'I know what you mean,' said Tracy. 'I told my mum I was gunna be a nun once just cause she wouldn't let me watch Bugs Bunny.'

Keith moved on to the next bundle.

'If they do split up,' said Tracy, 'which one'll you live with?'

Sometimes, thought Keith, even mates say the wrong thing.

'Or is that why you want the brochures,' continued Tracy, 'so you can choose the one who's planning to take the most interesting holidays? I'd pick the one who wants to go to Venice. I'd eat bricks to go to Venice. Or Peru. Or Melbourne.'

She slumped back against the bed and stared dreamily at a poster of the Victorian Arts Centre on the wall.

'Melbourne sounds great,' she said. 'Anywhere sounds great when you've never been further than Proserpine.'

Before Keith could explain that the brochures were for a second honeymoon for Mum and Dad so they could rediscover how deeply in love they were and never think about splitting up ever again, Tracy's mum came in with two cans of lemonade.

'Tracy ear-bashing you about her travel dreams, is she?' grinned Tracy's mum to Keith. She winked at Tracy.

'If you and Dad split up,' said Tracy, 'I'd pick Dad cause at least he'd go to Venice for the fishing.'

Keith nearly choked on a mouthful of lemonade. He wished Tracy would change the subject.

'I want to travel,' said Tracy's mum indignantly. 'When we've got a new roof and had the house re-stumped and saved up for an air-conditioner for the lounge, I'll be off for a week in Proserpine like a shot.'

'Rack off, you boring old chook,' said Tracy. Even though she and her mum were both grinning, Keith was shocked.

Dad called out the moment Keith stepped in through the fly screen door.

'Keith, in here.'

Mum and Dad were in the lounge, Mum on the settee next to the fan and Dad standing in the corner.

'Keith,' said Dad, 'we're very angry about the car.'

Keith looked at them.

They didn't look angry, they looked sad.

Mum's eyes were red and she'd rolled the *TV Times* into a tight tube and was gripping it with both hands. Her forehead was more corrugated than the dirt road out to Meninga.

Both corners of Dad's mouth were pointing to the floor and so were both his shoulders.

'We're very angry and disappointed,' said Dad.

'Is it the colours or the bumper bars or the spelling?' asked Keith in a small voice.

Dad's eyebrows went lower and now he did look angry.

'It's because you didn't discuss it with us first,' he said, his voice suddenly louder.

'I'm sorry,' said Keith miserably, 'I wanted to surprise you.'

'We know you did, love,' said Mum, 'and it was a lovely thought, but you should have talked to us about it first.'

'I can fix it up,' said Keith. 'If it's the Tropical Parrot and Hot Sunflower you don't like, I can fix that. Have a look at these, and I'll have it repainted any colour you like by the time you get back.'

He thrust a wad of holiday brochures at each of them.

'There's a great motel in Hobart,' he said as Mum and Dad stared at the brochures. 'It's on a hill and at this time of the year the winds down there have already started. It'll be freezing. You'll love it.'

Now they were both staring at him, mouths open.

'How about Adelaide?' said Keith. 'The Barossa

Valley's great for bush walks and crosswords and they get heaps of rain at this time of year.'

Dad stared at the brochures again and then at Keith again. 'For God's sake,' he said, 'we can't think about holidays, we've got a shop to run.'

'It's OK,' said Keith, 'I've worked it out. I'll take a couple of weeks off school and Tracy can help during the tea-time rush. She knows her way round a fish from going snorkelling with her dad. And Gino Morelli can help too, his dad used to run the aquarium in . . .'

'Keith,' Dad broke in, 'we are not going on any holiday.'

'It's a nice idea,' said Mum, 'but it's just not possible.'

'You've got to,' said Keith. 'How about a hang-gliding holiday in New Zealand? You go up to the snowfields in a helicopter, and you can bungy-jump too if you want.'

'We are not,' thundered Dad, 'going on holiday.'

'But you've got to,' pleaded Keith.

'Why have we?' asked Mum.

Keith took a deep breath. He had to say it.

'So you can stop talking about splitting up.'

There was a long silence.

Mum and Dad exchanged a look.

Keith's insides felt like they were in a spin-dryer.

Then Dad stepped forward and put his hands on Keith's shoulders and spoke slowly and softly.

'If you've heard us saying anything about splitting up, it's not what you think. We've been talking about splitting up in the shop, that's all.'

There was another long silence.

Keith struggled to work out what Dad meant, but his head felt like it was full of uncooked batter.

'What Dad's saying,' said Mum softly, 'is that the shop isn't making enough money so we've been talking about me getting a job outside the shop.'

Keith stared at her.

'That's right,' said Dad. 'Me and Mum don't like the idea, but the shop just isn't pulling in the trade, what with the new resort and the new snack bar in the pub.'

'We should have told you,' said Mum, 'but we were worried about how you'd feel because we know how much you like us working together.'

Suddenly Keith felt weak with relief. It was like having ninety kilos of ungutted cod lifted from his shoulders.

All the long faces and headaches and arguments and corrugated foreheads and droopy mouths hadn't been because anyone had stopped loving anyone.

They'd been because of a totally different problem.

A much easier one to solve.

Money.

FOUR

Keith put the coins into the slot and dialled.

'G'day,' said the wholesaler on the other end of the phone.

'This is Keith Shipley from the Paradise Fish Bar in Orchid Cove,' said Keith, 'and I'm in a phone box so I can't talk for long.'

'Do you want to place an order?' asked the wholesaler.

'No,' said Keith, 'I want to ask a favour.'

'I'm listening,' said the wholesaler.

'Well,' said Keith, 'our shop is operating in a pretty cut-throat business environment up here at the moment what with the new resort up the road and the new snack bar in the pub and it's really hard to make enough profit which is putting a serious strain on Mum and Dad, plus we're living in a small house with really thin walls so they can't even have sex that much so I was wondering if you could lower the price of your flour and oil a bit.'

There was a long pause at the other end.

'Is this a joke?' asked the wholesaler finally.

Don't be ridiculous, thought Keith. How could it be a joke? It's not even funny.

'It's an emergency,' said Keith, 'honest.'

'Look,' said the wholesaler, 'I'm operating in a pretty cut-throat business environment down here too. How would you like it if I rang you up at eight o'clock in the morning and went on about my financial problems?'

'You did,' said Keith. 'Last month.'

'Do your parents know you're doing this?' asked the wholesaler crossly.

'Sorry to bother you,' said Keith, and hung up.

He looked at the piece of paper with the phone numbers on it that he'd borrowed from the wall in the shop, and dialled again.

The potato distributor was even grumpier than the flour and oil wholesaler.

'Get nicked,' he said. 'Who do you think I am, Santa Claus?'

No chance of that, thought Keith, the only thing you've got in common with Santa Claus is a big bum.

He told the potato distributor that even a small price cut would help and that he himself had slashed his charge for peeling potatoes from five cents a potato to two cents, and the only reason he was charging Mum and Dad anything was that he had a car to repaint.

The potato wholesaler hung up.

Keith decided to try a different approach with the fish co-op.

At first it worked well.

Keith explained what he had in mind and the fish co-op man at the other end listened patiently even though Keith could hear people in the background yelling something about getting a move on and shifting some squid.

But when Keith had finished, the co-op man wasn't much help either. He explained that there wasn't any point in Keith getting up at three in the morning and coming down to the co-op with Tracy's dad's fish-gutting knife as all the fish were gutted on the boat. And anyway the co-op weren't allowed to give their fish-gutters cut-price fish as all the catch had to be sold at auction.

Keith asked if there was anything at the fish co-op that needed a paint job.

The man said 'fraid not.

Keith thanked him and hung up.

He felt panic bubbling up inside him.

It wasn't working.

Calm down, he told himself. Stop being a worry wart.

He took another deep breath.

It was time to tackle the problem face to face.

Keith found the pub owner in the bottle shop, hosing down the drive-through section.

'G'day young fella,' said the pub owner, hitching up his pyjama shorts, 'you've come to replace the compressor in my coolroom, have you?'

Keith remembered that the pub owner was famous throughout Orchid Cove for his sense of humour, which included putting blackcurrant syrup in blokes' beers when they weren't looking.

I want to ask you a favour,' said Keith.

'Fire away,' said the pub owner.

Keith explained how it would really improve the quality of Mum and Dad's lives if the pub owner could leave fish and chips off the menu in his new snack bar and replace them with liver and onions, say, or rissoles.

The pub owner laughed so hard he hosed himself on the leg.

What's so funny? thought Keith. I didn't mention blackcurrant syrup.

'Nice try, young fella,' said the pub owner. 'If you're passing the new resort could you drop in and tell them how much they'd improve the quality of my life if they'd stop selling beer. Replace it with tea, say, or flavoured milk.'

He started laughing again.

As Keith walked away he noticed the girder with the off-white paint on it where Mum had hit it with the car door.

Keith wished she'd hit it harder.

The foyer of the new resort was as big as a football pitch and the carpet smelled like deodorant.

Keith walked over to the reception desk.

'Excuse me,' he said to a woman who was tapping the keys of a computer with fingernails that matched her Hot Sunflower jacket. 'Could I see the manager please?'

'The manager's not in till nine,' said the woman. 'What was it in connection with?'

Keith explained it was to do with the fish and chips on their menu.

'Bistro, coffee shop or the Coral Room?' she asked.

'All of them,' said Keith.

'We don't have fish and chips in the Coral Room,' she said, glancing at a menu. 'We have Reef Fillets And Deep-Fried Potato Skins In A Basket With Mango And Oyster Mayonnaise. Did you want to make a complaint?'

Keith explained that he didn't want to make a complaint, he was just wondering if the fish and chips could be taken off the menus. He explained about Mum and Dad's financial difficulties.

The receptionist said she'd pass his request on to the manager.

As he was leaving though, he glanced back and saw her pointing him out to a man with the same colour jacket and a ponytail.

They were both sniggering.

All right for them, thought Keith angrily. They obviously haven't got depressed parents to look after.

Keith stared out the classroom window and wished Mr Gerlach would talk a bit more quietly when a person was trying to think.

He looked down at the list he'd made on the last page of his exercise book.

Ways For A Fish Shop To Earn Extra Money

1. Charge for salt.
2. Sell steamed veggies (not broccoli).
3. Let people dry their washing over the fryer.
4. Raffle the really big potato scallops.

Keith sighed. It wasn't a lot for a morning's hard thinking.

He started to write down the idea he'd just had about letting kids have a go of the chip-cutting machine for five cents a turn. Then he stopped. Even if a hundred kids a week did it, which would totally disrupt Dad's chip-cutting routine, it would still only bring in five dollars and at least one of the kids was bound to lop off a finger which would cost more than that in medical bills and needles and cotton.

Keith sighed again.

There must be other ways to get rich in Australia.

Only last week in geography Ms O'Connell had been saying that Australia was a vast country full of natural resources. Iron ore was one she'd mentioned a lot.

Keith was in the middle of wondering whether the Health Department would let a fish shop sell iron ore when Mr Gerlach's voice burst into his thoughts.

'Keith Shipley,' said Mr Gerlach. 'Could you see your way clear to sparing us a bit of your attention when I'm talking about your work?'

Keith looked up.

Mr Gerlach was holding up a painting that Keith had done in art.

'As I was saying, Mr Shipley, your use of texture around the chin and neck here, giving a sort of warty, rough appearance to the skin, suggests the person is a man and quite an old one, am I right?'

'No, sir,' said Keith, 'it's a cane toad.'

The class howled with laughter.

'It is, sir,' said Keith indignantly.

Mr Gerlach glared the class into silence, then took several steps towards Keith.

'You were told,' said Mr Gerlach angrily, 'to do a painting of a face.'

'It's a cane toad's face,' said Keith quietly, wishing he'd done Gary Murdoch like he'd first planned to.

Mr Gerlach sighed loudly and stared out the window.

'Being a teacher,' he said, 'is like walking across Australia. It's lonely, it's hard going, and every day you stub your toe on exactly the same thing.'

He turned back and looked at the class.

'Lumps of rock.'

He looked out the window again.

'Sometimes you think you see something glittering and you stop and pick it up.'

He turned and looked at Keith.

'But it's just another lump of rock.'

He looked at the class.

'You'd think we teachers'd give up, wouldn't you?'

The class nodded.

'But we don't, do you know why?'

The class shook their heads.

'Because,' said Mr Gerlach, 'we dream that one day, somewhere in this great land of ours, we'll come across a precious stone.'

There was a pause while Mr Gerlach looked sadly

at Keith's painting and Keith felt excitement rushing
through his veins.

'Excuse me, sir,' said Keith, 'What type of precious
stone?'

FIVE

'Opal,' said Tracy's dad, leaning back on his chair on the verandah and swatting at a mosquito.

'See, dummy,' said Tracy, elbowing Keith in the ribs and almost knocking him off the old vinyl settee, 'told you there's no diamonds in Australia.'

'All right,' said Keith, 'it was just an idea.'

He tried not to show how bitterly disappointed he felt.

If Mr Gerlach had answered his simple question instead of making the whole class paint cane toads, he wouldn't have spent the whole afternoon getting excited about starting up a diamond mine and buying Mum and Dad a mansion with fountains and really thick bedroom walls.

'There are a few diamonds around,' said Tracy's dad, 'but they're as scarce as bubble baths in a drought. Opal's the go in Australia. Worth almost as much as diamonds and twice as good to look at.'

Keith sat forward on the settee.

This was what he wanted to hear.

'Have you got any?' he asked.

'Me?' laughed Tracy's dad. 'If I had any I wouldn't keep 'em sitting round the house. I'd sell 'em and get that flamin' suspension on the car fixed.'

'You rat,' said Tracy. 'You'd spend the money on that heap of rust when your own daughter's never even been to Brisbane. You mean poop.'

To Keith's amazement Tracy's dad didn't frown and stop Tracy's pocket money and send her to her room. He just grinned and threw a boot at Tracy. She ducked and grinned back at him.

I must remember, thought Keith, to ask Tracy why her parents are so cheerful. Perhaps they drink.

'I knew a bloke once,' said Tracy's dad, 'who was tearing across the scrub in his truck and he hit a boulder and bust an axle. He was ropeable. Miles from anywhere, crook truck, no money for repairs. He gave the boulder an almightly kick . . .'

Keith could see it, vivid in his imagination. He couldn't stop himself. 'And the boulder split open,' he said, 'and it was a huge opal.'

Tracy and her dad rocked with laughter.

Keith felt his cheeks go hot with embarrassment.

'You should take up writing for the telly,' said Tracy's dad, grinning at him. 'What I was going to say was he kicked the rock, started walking towards town, got a lift with a couple of blokes on their way to the opal fields, went there with them, and in the next week picked up ninety thousand dollars worth of opal.'

Keith's cheeks were still hot, but now it was with excitement.

'Where exactly are these opal fields?' he asked.

Keith and Tracy lay on Tracy's bedroom floor looking up at the map of Australia stuck to her ceiling.

'See all those little black oval shapes?' said Tracy. 'They show where the opal fields are.'

Keith squinted up. He could see white squiggles (sheep), brown handlebars (cattle) and grey possum poos (iron ore), but he couldn't see any black ovals.

Tracy reached under her bed and pulled out a fishing rod. She pointed up with it, touching the map.

'See,' she said. 'There's some.'

Keith squinted.

Tracy reached under the bed again and handed Keith a pair of binoculars.

He focussed them on the bit of the map she was pointing to.

Black ovals.

Opal fields.

And they weren't that far away from Orchid Cove. Only about the width of Tracy's light shade.

He was so busy picturing Mum and Dad's delighted faces when they heard the news that he didn't realize for ages that his shoulder was touching Tracy's.

'You gunna do your geography assignment about opal instead of iron ore?' asked Tracy. 'Ms O'Connell'd have kittens. Even more than Mr Gerlach had today.'

'No,' said Keith, 'I'm not. I probably won't even be doing the geography assignment at all.'

There was a silence.

Tracy swivelled her head and looked at him.

'Don't let it get you down,' she said quietly. 'If your mum and dad want to split up there's nothing you can do about it.'

Keith looked at her. I really like you, he thought, but you've got some weird ideas.

Keith ran up the front steps. At the door he stopped and took a deep breath. The tropical smells hit his nose like fruit salad and new shoes and pineapple sherbert lollies all at once.

And there was another smell, from inside the house.

Spaghetti bolognese.

Nice one, thought Keith. Mum and Dad's favourite. Just the thing for them to be noshing while I tell them about our trip to the opal fields and the big house we'll be able to build up on the hill near Gary Murdoch's. With ninety-three taps. And six washers on each one. And a big verandah with a big table on it so we can sit around and tell jokes and laugh a lot.

Keith wondered if he should save the news till after dinner. People who broke into huge grins while they had mouths full of spaghetti bolognese tended to dribble down their fronts.

Won't matter, he thought. We'll have a washing machine soon.

He went in.

He couldn't hear the clatter of forks on plates, which meant they probably hadn't started. Dad would probably be at the sink doing the salad. Mum would probably be at the cupboard getting out the plates. The spaghetti bolognese would probably be on the table, steaming.

He'd tell them straight away and they'd turn to him, eyes shining through the steam.

He reached the kitchen.

And stopped.

Mum wasn't at the cupboard, she was standing gripping the fridge with both hands, face pale with anger, forehead criss-crossed with furrows.

Dad wasn't at the sink, he was standing with his back pressed against the window, face pale with shock, mouth drooping almost past his chin.

The spaghetti bolognese wasn't steaming on the table.

It was sliding down the wall next to Dad.

Keith looked at Mum again, then Dad, then the bolognese.

A cold lump was sliding down the inside of Keith's ribs at exactly the same speed as the meat sauce and bits of spaghetti were sliding down the wall.

Mum stepped forward and picked up the pot from the floor.

'Sorry love,' she said quietly to Keith. 'I lost my temper. I'll do you some sausages.'

'I'll do them,' said Dad.

Keith watched Mum and Dad avoid each other's eyes.

The sooner we're rich the better, he thought.

Keith told Mum and Dad about the opals after they'd all cleaned up the kitchen and had their sausages.

They listened carefully while he repeated Tracy's dad's truck story and explained how opals were almost as valuable as diamonds and told them that he'd checked the map and knew where to find some.

Dad turned the telly off.

They're not smiling, thought Keith. Perhaps it's shock. He'd seen a geezer in a film once who'd won the pools and had just turned grey and fainted into a rice pudding.

He was glad when Dad was safely sitting down again.

'Look Keith,' said Dad softly. 'We've got problems, I'm not denying that.'

'Financial problems,' said Mum.

'But,' said Dad, 'we're not going to solve them with crazy schemes.'

'You're a good kid,' said Mum, 'and we appreciate what you're trying to do, love, but Dad's right. Now come on, you've got school tomorrow, time to hit the sack. We'll talk about it some more in the morning.'

Even before Keith had left the room he knew it was pointless.

Some people just weren't capable of solving their own problems.

Some people had to have everything done for them.

Keith tapped softly on Tracy's window.

He listened.

All he could hear were the dawn cries of the birds in the forest at the back of Tracy's place.

He tapped again.

Suddenly there was a snuffling and snorting but it wasn't Tracy waking up, it was her dog Buster sniffing round Keith's school bag.

'Shhhh,' said Keith.

38

Buster looked as though he was about to bark.

Keith grabbed him round the mouth.

That's probably how you lost the leg and half the ear, thought Keith. Harassing friends of Tracy's who urgently need to speak to her.

Buster sneezed and Tracy opened her window.

She stared at Keith.

'Don't squeeze his mouth,' she said, 'he's got sore teeth.'

Once Keith was safely inside and Buster was in the corner contentedly chewing on Tracy's binoculars, Keith explained to Tracy that he needed to borrow a map showing how to get to the opal fields.

Tracy grinned. 'They agreed to go. Ripper.'

'No,' said Keith, 'they didn't. I'm going by myself.'

She looked at him.

Please, he thought, don't try and talk me out of it.

She didn't.

She stood on her bed and unstuck the map from the ceiling. Then she said three things that made Keith wish she was coming with him.

The first was that she wished she could go with him, but she'd promised her folks she'd never run away again after the time she'd tried to catch a bus to Melbourne when she was seven.

The second was how he'd need some extra money. She took all the notes and coins out of her cane toad money box and pressed them into his hand.

He started to say no, then remembered that all he had left of his own money was two dollars and eleven cents.

The third thing she whispered very close to his ear while she was holding the window up so he could climb out.

'Be careful you dopey mongrel.'

SIX

The first bit was easy.

Keith caught the early bus into Cairns along with an assortment of workers, backpackers and schoolkids.

The only dodgy moment was when he realized that the woman sitting two seats in front of him was Mrs Newman's grown-up daughter Gail.

Don't turn round, he thought.

It was the first telepathic message he'd sent for a while, but it worked.

She hobbled off the bus at Cairns Hospital without once glancing back.

Poor thing, thought Keith. When I've struck it rich I'll send her some money so she can take her family to live somewhere cooler where her feet won't swell up. That motel in Hobart perhaps.

At the bus station in Cairns things got more difficult.

Keith knew that any minute Mum and Dad would be waking up and going into his room and seeing his empty bed and finding his note.

And even though the note said not to worry because he'd be back soon with the opals and could they start talking to some builders, Keith was pretty sure they'd ring the police.

41

He had to move quickly.

Except there wasn't a bus that went all the way to the opal fields. Not the ones he wanted to go to, the ones Tracy had circled on the map, the ones where Tracy's dad's friend had struck it rich.

And even if he went as close as he could by bus, which wasn't very close, he'd use up nearly all his money on the ticket.

Keith stood back from the ticket window, desperately trying to think what to do.

If he started hitch-hiking this close to home the police would probably pick him up.

If he went to a bank and asked for a loan the bank manager would probably want to speak to Mum and Dad.

If he caught a taxi and offered the driver half the opals he was going to find, he'd probably have to hand over the other half to get back.

Then he saw it.

Across the road.

A big double-decker tourist bus with a crowd of tourists clambering aboard.

The destination window on the front of the bus said Brisbane, which meant it was going south.

It was a start.

Keith hurried across the road, waited until the driver had his head in the baggage compartment, then slipped aboard in the middle of a large family.

He went upstairs and sat near the front so he wouldn't look as though he was hiding.

Just as the bus was moving off, three women with white hair and T-shirts came upstairs and one of them sat next to him.

'Hey,' she said with an American accent, 'you just join the tour?'

Keith nodded.

Please, he thought, please don't be a retired FBI agent.

'Where are your folks?' asked the woman.

'Back there,' said Keith, pointing towards Orchid Cove.

No point in making up stories, she probably had a lie-detector machine in her overnight bag.

The woman glanced at the large family at the back of the bus and winked at Keith.

'More fun up the front, right?' she grinned. 'Hey, you should have been with us yesterday. We went to . . . what was it called?'

'Orchid Cove,' said her friend.

'Orchid Cove,' said the woman. 'A tropical paradise.'

Keith nodded politely. You wouldn't be saying that if you had your parents with you, he thought.

Then he noticed the plastic shopping bag the woman was holding on her lap.

Printed on it were the words *Ollie's Opals And Gifts, Duty Free Available*.

'Have you got any opals in there?' asked Keith.

'Sure have,' said the woman. 'Wanna peek?'

She rummaged in the bag, pulled out a wad of tissue paper, unfolded it and held up a thin metal chain.

Hanging from it, set in a clasp, was a small black stone.

'Twelve hundred dollars,' said the woman, 'but I got it for eleven hundred and fifty.'

As Keith stared, the bus jolted and the opal started to spin. Colours flashed from deep inside it. Tropical Parrot. Hot Sunflower. Charcoal Red. Pacific Blue. Frothy Orange. Dusky Pink. Vatican Purple.

Blimey, thought Keith, I've seen whole colour charts that haven't had this many colours in them.

And he'd never seen colours so bright, not even on picnics when he closed his eyes in the sun and pressed bread rolls into his eye sockets.

Later, after the woman had dozed off, Keith stared out the bus window and thought about how many opals he'd be able to fit into his school bag.

A million dollars worth at least.

Suddenly even the colours of the trees and houses and glimpses of ocean flashing past seemed brighter.

The bus slowed down as it went through a town and Keith, wrestling with Tracy's map, realized it was the town where he had to get off to go inland to the opal fields.

He folded the map frantically.

How could he stop a bus without drawing attention to himself?

Even as he was trying to choose between telepathy and nudging the sleeping American woman so she slumped on to the emergency buzzer, he saw that they were passing a road junction.

44

His turn-off.

He jumped to his feet.

He'd just have to go down and tell the driver that he was sorry but he'd got on the wrong bus after receiving a blow to the head playing softball.

Then the bus pulled into a service station.

Amazing, thought Keith. I've just stopped a bus with telepathy and I didn't even know I was doing it.

'Morning tea,' said the American woman's friend.

'Look at you,' said the American woman to Keith. 'On your feet already. You must have done this trip before.'

Keith grabbed his school bag and hurried back to the stairs and stepped into the middle of the large family and clattered down with them and off the bus.

He realized he was shaking.

With luck like this, he thought, when I get to the opal field I might have to buy a second school bag.

In the service station cafe Keith bought two postcards and went into the toilets and locked himself in a cubicle.

While he waited for the bus to leave he wrote the postcards.

Dear Mum and Dad,

This is just to let you know that I took the torch, the hammer, the gardening trowel, the plastic strainer, the chocolate biscuits, and the stuff that's missing from the bathroom and my clothes drawer. So it's O K, you haven't been burgled. I'm fit and well. Please don't worry, things are looking even better than I thought opal-wise.

    Love, Keith.

    Dear Tracy,
    Wish you were here.
    Keith.
    PS. I O U $24.35.
    (signed) Keith Shipley.
    PPS. Thanks.

Then he ate four chocolate biscuits.

At last he heard the bus revving away into the distance.

He went back into the café for a milkshake. The mid-morning news was just starting on a TV on the wall.

Keith froze.

What if there was a nationwide alert out for him and his photo appeared on the screen?

There might even be a reward.

The other customers would jump him.

He wouldn't stand a chance.

And he'd just ordered a milkshake so he couldn't leave without looking obvious.

Keith stared at the screen, holding his breath.

The Prime Minister in Canberra.

Floods in Bangladesh.

Cockatoos playing chess in Gympie.

Then it was over.

46

Keith sat down for a minute and let relief and milk-shake flood through him.

Funny though, he thought, that there isn't a nation-wide search yet. Police must be double checking that Mum and Dad aren't loonies.

Keith finished his milkshake and started walking back towards the road junction.

One good thing about the police not looking for him yet, he could hitch a lift. And in a friendly country like Australia he'd get one in no time.

Keith put on his friendliest face as the car turned off the highway and headed towards him.

He stuck out his hand with his thumb pointing towards the opal fields and tried to look like someone who was not only great at conversation but didn't make smells in cars.

The car roared past.

Keith closed his eyes as the dust billowed around him.

He felt dizzy and weak.

He looked at his watch, squinting in the glare of the sun.

Nearly four hours he'd been standing there.

Eighteen vehicles.

What was the matter with people? He didn't look like a murderer or a terrorist.

He rubbed some more sun-block cream on his face and adjusted the knotted T-shirt on his head.

If he didn't have something to eat or drink soon the nineteenth vehicle would be an ambulance.

He picked up his school bag and plodded slowly back towards the service station.

It was the most beautiful sight he'd seen since arriving in Australia, including Orchid Cove beach at sunset and mango ice-cream.

It was parked next to the service station café and Keith felt like running over and kissing it.

He didn't because if you were trying to keep a low profile it was best not to be seen kissing a semi-trailer with a bulldozer on the back.

It wasn't the battered truck itself that made Keith's spirits pick themselves up and do a little dance, or the dust-covered bulldozer. It was the South Australian number plates.

If the truck was heading home it would be going inland, south-west, through the opal fields.

Keith went into the cafe.

He held his breath.

Nobody jumped on him and yelled for a reward, so the nationwide search obviously still hadn't started.

He asked the man behind the counter if he knew who was driving the truck with the bulldozer on the back.

'I am,' said a voice.

Keith turned.

The truck driver, a big man with earrings, was eating sausages and eggs and watching *Play School* on TV.

'Are you going inland towards South Australia?' asked Keith.

'Yep,' said the truck driver.

'Could I have a lift please?' asked Keith.

'Nope,' said the truck driver.

There was a long pause filled only by the sound of Big Ted building a suspension bridge out of cornflakes packets.

'Company policy,' said the truck driver. 'No lifts.'

'Anyway,' said the man behind the counter, 'aren't you a bit young? Where's your parents.'

'Back there,' said Keith, pointing towards Orchid Cove.

He hurried outside.

I bet if you read that company policy carefully, thought Keith, it says no lifts *in* the truck, not no lifts *on* the truck.

He looked around.

No one was watching.

He climbed on to the back of the truck, opened the bulldozer cabin door, crawled in, closed the door, and lay on the cabin floor hugging his school bag.

Keith lay there, by his calculation, through the rest of *Play School*, all of *Danger Mouse*, and some of *Gumby*.

Then the truck door slammed and the engine roared and they started to move.

Keith tried to make himself as small as he could. He pressed his cheek to the metal floor and the vibrations through his cheekbone made him see stars.

He closed his eyes and imagined each exploding point of light was an opal.

SEVEN

'All right you – out.'

Keith sat up, cold and dazed and aching.

Something was different.

The vibrations had stopped.

So had his dream. He'd been on a yacht with Mum and Dad, a luxury yacht with built-in fish fryers and solid opal taps.

The man with the earrings and the scowl hadn't been on the yacht.

He was here now though, glaring at Keith.

'I said no lifts,' growled the man.

For a moment Keith wondered if the man was a lift operator, then remembered he was a truck driver.

A pang of fear gripped Keith just before the truck driver did.

Keith grabbed his school bag as the truck driver dragged him out of the bulldozer and down off the back of the truck.

He staggered and blinked. The sun was just coming up over the horizon.

'Where are we?' asked Keith as his teeth started to chatter.

'Twelve hours inland,' said the truck driver. 'Which means it'll take you about twelve weeks to walk back.'

Keith looked around. It was the country all right, but there weren't any trees, just bushes and dry grass.

And concrete. He was standing on a square of concrete with two petrol pumps on it, and a small fibro office to one side.

'Is this the opal fields?' asked Keith, struggling to control his teeth.

'Opal fields?' said the truck driver, with a snort of laughter. 'They're four hours further on. If you start now you should get there in four weeks.'

'Leave him alone, Col,' said a voice.

Keith turned and saw another man with a plump face and dirty orange overalls coming over from the office.

'He's only a kid,' said the other man.

'Still could have got me the sack,' said Col.

'Get lost,' said the other man. 'When was the last time you saw an inspector out here?'

'Could happen,' muttered Col.

The other man turned to Keith.

'You on your own?' he asked.

Keith took a deep breath, sent his teeth a stern telepathic message, and told the two men about Mum and Dad's financial problems.

Col leant against the truck and rubbed his face in his hands and listened gravely.

The other man looked at Keith and then at the ground and then back at Keith.

They're sympathetic, thought Keith. They can see I can't afford to waste time and they're going to help me.

52

He'd just finished thinking that when they took him across and locked him in the office.

Keith sat in a cracked vinyl swivel chair and stared gloomily at a model train on a shelf on the office wall.

Outside he could hear Col and the other man arguing about him.

'It'd only be till tonight, Mick, the cops'd be here before dark,' said Col.

'You can't leave him here,' said Mick. 'I'm not having the cops coming out here. I've got an unregistered tow truck out the back and six microwaves I'm looking after for someone.'

'Well I can't take him to the cops,' said Col, 'not with the state of my log-book.'

Keith wondered what the wages would be like in prison. Probably take twenty years to earn enough for a yacht.

He wondered if Tracy would come and visit him.

He wondered what she'd say if she was here now.

'Jeez, you're a worry wart,' that's what she'd say.

Suddenly he knew what he had to do.

He went and banged on the office door as loudly as he could.

'Col, Mick,' he shouted. 'Open up a sec.'

The door flew open and the two men stood there, looking at him.

'Col,' said Keith, 'if you take me to the opal fields I'll paint your truck.'

Col stared at him.

'And the bulldozer too if you want,' said Keith. 'I'm

53

good at it, I've done a car and a fish and chip shop.'

Col and Mick exchanged a glance.

Col sighed.

Mick grinned.

Col stared at the horizon and rubbed the back of his neck for about a minute.

'All right,' said Col, 'paint my truck and if it's any good I'll take you as far as the opal fields.'

'Thanks,' said Keith, 'you won't regret it.'

'Get him some paint, Mick,' said Col.

Keith went over and walked round the truck. It was at least twelve times bigger than the Corolla.

This could take all day, he thought. Hope they've got a big brush.

Mick came over and handed Keith a cardboard box.

Inside were some tiny tins of hobby paint and some skinny little brushes.

Keith stared at them.

'I build model trains,' said Mick sheepishly.

Keith looked up at the truck towering over him.

That's all I need, he thought. Stranded in the bush with a couple of loonies.

'I won't get half a bumper bar done with these,' he said. He spoke softly so as not to startle Mick and cause him to have a fit or a violent outburst or something.

Col appeared and handed Keith a piece of plywood.

'There you go,' he said, 'you can do it on that.' He went and stood next to the truck. 'Is this a good place for me to stand?'

Suddenly Keith understood.

Col didn't want him to paint the truck, he wanted him to paint a picture of the truck.

Mick brought a wooden crate for Keith to sit on, which was just as well because Keith's knees had suddenly gone a bit wobbly.

It wasn't that Keith didn't like painting pictures, he did.

But every time he painted one something seemed to go wrong.

At school Mr Gerlach had kittens.

At home Mum and Dad got tense and unhappy just because a couple of times Keith had left tubes of paint on the settee with the tops off and Dad had sat on them.

OK, said Keith to himself, stop being a worry wart. Mr Gerlach isn't here. Mum and Dad aren't here. There's just me and Mick in the office and Col standing over there sticking his chest out.

'Behind the wheel might be better,' Keith told Col.

Col climbed up into the cab.

Keith picked up a stub of a pencil and started sketching the truck on to the plywood.

He'd be OK as long as it didn't end up looking like a cane toad.

'Finished yet?' called Col. 'My arms have gone numb.'

'Nearly,' said Keith. 'Hang on.'

Just a few more dabs of Burnt Ochre on Col's cowboy hat and . . .

'OK,' said Keith, 'finished.'

Col climbed stiffly down from the cab, rubbing his arms, and looked at the painting.

Keith crossed his fingers and hoped Col's mum and dad had taken him to lots of art galleries when he was a kid.

If he likes the colour of the truck, thought Keith, I'm probably OK.

It had been a big risk, changing the colour of the truck to purple, but off-white wouldn't have shown up as well against the gold and silver sunrise. He'd thought at first of making the truck orange, but that would have clashed with the blue snake wrapped around the black bulldozer.

If he likes the snake, thought Keith, I'm probably OK.

He peeped up at Col's face.

Col was frowning.

'It's flying,' he said. 'The truck's flying.'

'That's right,' said Keith. 'I've painted it from the point of view of a truck inspector as you roar out of the sunrise over his head.'

'What are those things flying around the truck?' asked Col.

'Vampire bats,' said Keith.

'What's that gleam coming from Col's mouth?' asked Mick, who'd come over from the office.

'An opal tooth,' said Keith.

Col slowly broke into a grin.

'It's a beauty,' he said to Keith. 'Let's go.'

He gave Keith a leg-up into the cab, said hooroo to Mick, gunned the motor and they were off.

While they bounced along the dusty road Keith told Col about South London and how big trucks from Europe used to get wedged under the pub overhang coming round the corner from Pontifract Road.

Col told Keith about the Birdsville Track and how once he'd hit a pot-hole so big he'd lost three hundred fan heaters and the can of drink he was holding at the time.

Then the vibrations from the road started to make Keith feel drowsy and he closed his eyes and thought about the opal fields and wondered if they really were fields or if they were just called that because the glittering opals were in rows like strawberries.

EIGHT

Keith snapped awake.

Col was leaning across him, pushing open the door of the cab.

'Is this the opal fields?' croaked Keith, squinting through the dusty windscreen.

'Yep,' said Col.

All Keith could see was dust.

The only things glinting were Col's eyes as he looked up at Keith's painting, which he'd stuck to the roof of the cab with muffler tape.

'She's a ripper,' he said. 'Blokes at the depot'll chuck their guts when they see it.'

'Thanks,' said Keith.

He grabbed his school bag and jumped down from the cab.

The heat hit him in the face like Mr Gerlach's breath after a curry lunch.

'Don't forget,' said Col, 'if the cops pick you up, leave me out of it.'

'O.K,' said Keith.

Col gunned the motor and the truck started to move off.

'And give your folks a ring,' he yelled.

'I'm going to,' shouted Keith, waving.

And I am, he thought, as he watched the truck disappear down the dirt road, just as soon as I've got the opals.

He looked at the ground around him.

It certainly wasn't a field. More a piece of desert with tyre tracks and a few wispy bits of dry grass.

And no opals to be seen.

They must be in the dust.

He dropped to his knees, opened his school bag, and felt around in the thick orange powder.

Nothing.

Just dust.

Then he touched something small and round and hard.

He picked it up and blew the dust off it.

It sparkled.

Heart pounding, he rubbed it on his jeans.

This one opal, he thought, could pay for the plumbing in our new house, or a month's holiday for Mum and Dad in a balloon, or a fishing boat so we can catch our own fish, or a Rolls Royce with speed stripes, or a . . .

The opal had stopped sparkling.

Keith saw why.

It had been wrapped in silver paper, which Keith had shredded with his rubbing.

And it wasn't an opal at all, it was a piece of old bubblegum.

Keith tossed it away.

OK, he said to himself, be sensible. You're not

going to find opals lying here by the side of the road. Any opals here would have been picked up years ago by people driving to the shops who remembered they'd left their money at home and needed a couple of precious stones to pay for the groceries.

Keith stood up and looked around.

Now the dust from the truck had settled, he could see he was in the middle of a vast, flat plain with hardly anything sprouting out of it.

Anything green, that is.

There were other things, brown things, most of them taller than Keith, dotted over the landscape for as far as he could see.

Piles of dirt.

Keith had a horrible suspicion he knew what they were.

Keith decided to check out the town first and buy some cans of drink because he'd seen a movie once where some prospectors had run out of water in the desert and had got dehydrated and started seeing piles of gold that were really donkeys.

All he could see were two buildings and a caravan park.

'Excuse me,' he said to a man climbing into a four wheel drive, 'where's the town?'

The man grinned and knocked some dust out of his beard with his hat.

'You're standing in it,' he said.

Keith looked at the buildings.

One was a pub with cement brick walls and a corrugated iron roof and a wooden verandah and a huge dirt car-park.

The other was a shop with fibro walls and a corrugated iron roof and a wooden verandah and a huge dirt car-park.

Over the shop door was a sign saying *Curly's Store*.

I hope Curly sells cold drinks, thought Keith as he went in.

When his eyes got used to the gloom, he saw that Curly sold everything. Food, hardware, clothes, make-up, camping gear, kitchen utensils, dog care products, and that was just on the first shelf Keith looked at.

Curly also sold newspapers.

Keith held his breath while he checked to see if any of the headlines said NATIONWIDE SEARCH FOR BRAVE OPAL BOY.

They didn't.

Keith felt relieved, but with a twinge of disappointment. Then he saw that the papers were three days old.

'Can I help you?' said a gruff voice.

Standing behind the counter was an elderly man wearing an off-white T-shirt with *Curly* printed on it. He was completely bald.

That's a bit rough, thought Keith, giving a person a nickname just cause he's got hairy arms.

Keith bought three cans of drink and a meatloaf sandwich. Once the sandwich was in his mouth he realized how ravenous he was and bought two more.

Then he got down to business.

'Those piles of dirt,' asked Keith, 'are they . . . ?'

'Mullock dumps,' said Curly, slapping a piece of meatloaf on to a piece of bread, 'from the diggings.'

'How long does it take to dig an opal mine?' asked Keith, dreading the answer.

'If you've got a diesel drill and some gelignite,' said Curly, 'you can get a decent shaft down in a day. By hand it takes weeks.'

Keith felt a lump in his stomach that wasn't meatloaf.

'You don't happen to know of any spare mines around here, do you?' he asked. 'Ones where the owners have struck it rich and gone to Disneyland.'

Curly gave Keith a look that made him think Curly must have once had a bad experience at Disneyland.

'We've got a rule out here,' said Curly. 'You never touch another bloke's mine. Never.'

'What happens if you do?' asked Keith in a small voice, hoping he sounded like he was doing this for a school project.

Curly reached under the counter.

Keith wondered if he was going to produce a school project kit.

But it wasn't a cardboard folder that Curly thumped down on to the counter.

It was a big, black, double-barrelled shotgun.

Keith stood on the store verandah, swallowed his last bit of meatloaf sandwich, and looked around for a good place to fossick.

When Curly had first mentioned the word fossick,

Keith had feared it was a technical term meaning to dig up opals with a bulldozer and a dump truck.

Then Curly had explained that it simply meant picking up opals by hand on the surface rather than digging down for them, and that just as many opals were found by fossickers as by the crazies who sank shafts half way to Belgium.

Keith spotted a good place to fossick.

Keith looked at his watch and sighed.

Ten forty-three.

He'd been on his hands and knees in the pub car-park for twenty-five minutes in the scorching sun and all he'd found, apart from a few thousand stones and rocks and a few hundred cigarette butts and beer bottle tops, was a bleached bone from a small animal or lizard.

He sighed again.

When opal miners got drunk and spun their tyres, they obviously jumped out of the car afterwards to check for opals.

He looked at his watch again.

Ten forty-four.

He'd planned to find all the opals he needed by twelve-thirty so he could organise a charter plane to get him back to Orchid Cove in time for dinner.

He looked at the bleached bone again.

Maybe it wasn't part of a lizard.

Maybe it was part of a barbecued chicken.

Or a fossicker.

Keith decided to try somewhere else.

*

Keith looked at his watch and sighed.

Eleven twenty-seven.

He'd been on his hands and knees in the caravan park for thirty-eight minutes in the scorching sun and all he'd found was a shoelace and a plastic hose nozzle.

It wasn't much of a caravan park, just a square of dust with a dozen or so battered caravans, but he'd hoped the van wheels might have stirred up the odd gem or two.

Nothing.

A voice broke into his thoughts.

'Scuse me.'

It belonged to a middle-aged woman in a fluffy dressing-gown.

Keith thought she must be melting. He was wearing a T-shirt and he felt like a chip in oil.

'While you're down there, love,' she said, 'could you do me a favour? Keep an eye out for a filling. Merv threw up on his way back from the pub last night and lost one.'

Keith said that normally he'd be happy to, but he'd just decided to try somewhere else.

Keith looked at his watch.

He didn't have the energy to sigh.

Nineteen minutes past twelve.

He'd been on his hands and knees by the petrol pumps at the side of Curly's store for nearly an hour in the scorching sun and all he'd found was a tyre valve and three pieces of old bubblegum.

So much for his theory that when truck drivers stopped for diesel and jumped down from their cabs, the heels of their cowboy boots would gouge out opals.

Keith pulled the knotted T-shirt off his head and wiped the dust and sweat off his face.

This is hopeless, he thought.

Not just this spot, the whole trip.

Coming all this way had been a stupid waste of time, thirty-two hours of worry and discomfort and knots in the guts, all for nothing.

The only good bit had been painting Col's truck.

Keith looked round for a phone box so he could ring Mum and Dad and tell them he was coming home as soon as a truck came past that would swap him a lift for a painting.

He had a vision of Mum and Dad's faces glowing with relief at his safe return.

Then he saw the disappointment gradually furrowing Mum's forehead and drooping Dad's mouth as they realized he hadn't brought any opals.

Disappointment closely followed by migraines and upset tummies and crosswords and solitary bush walks and arguments and . . .

Keith stood up and went into the store.

NINE

'Noodling,' said Curly, slapping a piece of meatloaf on to a piece of bread.

Keith lowered his lemonade and stared at him. Noodling?

What did spaghetti have to do with finding opals?

'Sifting through the mullock dumps,' said Curly. 'Picking up bits of colour the shafties have missed. Best way to fossick.'

Of course, thought Keith, his body suddenly tingling and not just from the lemonade or the sunburn. That's where I've been going wrong. No noodling.

'One important thing to remember when you choose a dump,' said Curly, handing him the sandwich. 'If there's someone working the shaft, make sure you ask their permission. And even if a shaft looks deserted, don't go down it.'

'Don't worry,' said Keith through a mouthful of meatloaf, 'I won't.'

What was the point of going down a mine, finding opals worth hundreds of thousands of dollars and then spending most of it on having shotgun pellets surgically removed?

'You won't find big stuff like this in the mullocks,' said Curly, thumping a big dirty rock on to the counter, 'but you might pick up some of these.' He rattled a jam jar half full of tiny dirty rocks.

Keith stared at the dirty rocks to make sure he wasn't seeing things.

Yes, they were definitely dirty rocks.

So that's why Curly was called Curly. It wasn't his arm-hairs, it was his brain.

'Thanks for the advice,' said Keith, backing towards the door, 'and they're great-looking rocks, but I've only got room in my bag for opals.'

Curly grinned for the first time since Keith had met him.

Oh no, thought Keith, here's where he grabs his shotgun and runs amok.

But instead Curly rubbed some of the dirt off the big rock and held it up in front of a window. Colours flashed out of it.

'Never looks much till it's cut and polished,' said Curly.

Keith went over and took the rock from him and ran his fingers over the rough sandstone and the smooth ribbons of flashing opal running through it.

Suddenly he didn't feel exhausted any more.

He couldn't wait to get out on the mullock dumps and start sifting through the dirty rocks and sorting out which ones were opals.

'Thanks very much,' he said to Curly, handing him the rock. 'You've made a troubled family very happy.'

He headed for the door.

'Just a sec,' said Curly. 'Talking about families, where's yours?'

Keith froze.

He forced his mouth open to tell Curly the story he'd made up earlier that morning, the one about Mum and Dad being kidnapped by Taiwanese pirates who were demanding a ransom of opals and potato scallops, but suddenly it didn't seem like such a good story.

He tried to make up another one, but his brain had turned to dust.

Helplessly he pointed in what he thought was the direction of Orchid Cove.

'Good-o,' said Curly, 'they're in the caravan park. Just checking they're not camped on my claim.'

Keith looked at his watch and sighed.

Two thirty-three.

He'd been squatting on this mullock heap with the scorching wind blowing dust into his eyes and mouth for over an hour and a half.

He must have sifted tonnes of dirt through Mum's plastic strainer.

He'd smashed hundreds of dirty rocks with Dad's hammer.

Nothing.

He looked across at the next heap where an Aboriginal family were systematically sifting the dirt and chatting and laughing.

'How ya goin?' one of the women called across to him.

'Not very well,' Keith shouted back.

'Don't give up,' yelled the woman, 'we found heaps in there last week.'

*

Keith looked at his watch and coughed.

Twenty past four.

This second dump was no better. He must have sifted just about the whole thing, most of it in the plastic strainer and the rest in his mouth, and he hadn't found a single opal.

Plus there was the whine.

The opal fields were noisy enough, with generators and drills clattering away, but coming from behind the next dump was a high-pitched whine that made concentrating on finding opals impossible.

Keith couldn't stand it any longer.

He threw down his trowel and strainer and stormed over the next dump towards the whine.

As soon as he got over the top he saw what it was.

A small generator strapped to a tent on legs.

Keith went over and tapped the tent on the shoulder.

A flap opened and a man's face, eerily lit by a purple light, peered out.

'Excuse me, but do you have to make so much noise?' said Keith.

'Sorry,' said the man. 'Ultraviolet light. Shows up the opal.'

'Have you found any?' asked Keith.

'Absolutely,' said the man. 'Last week.'

'Well it's nice to know there's some around,' said Keith. 'I'd just about given up on that heap over there.'

'You won't find any over there,' said the man.

'Why not?' asked Keith.

'Because,' said the man, 'I did that yesterday.'

Keith dropped his school bag and wiped the sweat off his face.

At last he'd found one.

A mullock heap that hadn't been noodled in the last week.

In fact this one had wisps of dry grass growing on it so perhaps it had never been noodled at all.

Fat chance.

But he had to keep trying.

There was an old caravan by the dump so Keith banged on the door and called out to see if anyone was home.

No one was.

He went over to the shaft and yelled down it.

No one answered.

Then he noticed the sign.

Keep Out. Private Claim. By Order Of C. Kovacs, General Store.

Blimey, thought Keith, this must be Curly's mine.

Then another thought came to him. With Curly back at the store, this was his chance to check out an opal mine without getting shot.

He shone his torch down the shaft, but couldn't even see the bottom.

Keith knew he had to go down.

Just for a look.

Above the shaft was a winch with a coil of thick

wire. Keith uncoiled the wire and it slithered down into the darkness.

When it went slack he knew it had touched the bottom. He put the torch in his mouth, gripped the wire with both hands, planted the soles of his feet against the sides of the shaft and half climbed, half slid down in a shower of dirt and rock fragments.

The bottom of the shaft was cool and dark.

He shone the torch around. There was a tunnel running off to one side, high enough to walk along.

Keith didn't.

He gazed for a while at the walls of the tunnel, at the bands and seams of rock running along it. Some looked hard, some looked crumbly, and any one of them could have been stuffed with opal.

But he didn't touch.

He didn't want to be a thief.

He wanted to be a miner.

Curly stared at Keith, the lump of meatloaf and the slice of bread in his hands forgotten.

'Paint my store?'

'That's right,' said Keith. 'I'll paint your store in return for a day down your mine. As long as I can keep everything I find down there.'

Curly thought about this for a long time.

'There's not much down there,' he said. 'I've given up on it.'

Oh yeah, thought Keith, so why have you got a big Keep Out sign plastered all over it?

'I'll pay for the paint,' said Keith.

He'd already seen a paintbox for eleven dollars fifty on the stationery shelf and a big drawing pad for three dollars.

That was nearly all the money he had left but it was worth it.

'Are you any good?' asked Curly.

'I did a truck on the way here and the owner was delighted,' said Keith.

Curly thought some more.

'OK,' he said, 'it's a deal. Paint this place and you can have full use of my claim for twenty-four hours.'

They shook hands.

'I'll do it tomorrow,' said Keith.

'You'd better buy the paint now,' said Curly, 'because I'm away on business most of tomorrow.'

Keith went to the stationery shelf and grabbed the paintbox and pad.

When he got back to the counter he saw that Curly was over at the other side of the store doing a sum on his fingers.

'I reckon,' said Curly, 'you'll need about twenty litres to do the outside of this place. That'll be a hundred and eighty-five dollars please.'

TEN

The first half-litre was the hardest.

Keith knocked on the door of the first caravan and a man in off-white underpants appeared. He looked like he'd just woken up.

'Sorry to disturb you so early,' said Keith, 'but have you got any old paint to spare? I'm painting Curly's store.'

The man stared at him.

'Not a picture,' Keith added, 'the store itself.' He thought he'd better get that straight as it could be a bit confusing.

'Why doesn't Curly supply the paint?' growled the man.

'He's supplying the step-ladder and the dust sheets,' said Keith, 'and I'm supplying the paint.'

'Why?' growled the man.

'It's a long story,' said Keith, 'but it involves raising money for a very worthy cause.'

'What worthy cause?' growled the man.

'Well,' said Keith, 'my mum and dad have got this fish and chip shop way over on the coast and the hotel has just started up a snack bar and the new resort round on the headland has got three restaurants and . . .'

'Hang on,' grunted the man.

He went inside the van and Keith heard him clattering about. He came back with a litre tin of paint, handed it to Keith and closed the door.

'Thanks,' Keith called out.

He opened the tin with the claw end of Dad's hammer. The tin was half full of dull red anti-rust paint.

Nice one, thought Keith. Only nineteen-and-a-half litres to go.

The door of the second caravan swung open and the middle-aged woman in the fluffy dressing-gown smiled at Keith.

'It's OK, love,' she said, 'we found it. I superglued it back in and he's eaten steak on it and everything.'

Keith explained that he hadn't come about the filling, he'd come about paint.

'Merv,' she called into the van, 'dig out that aquamarine gloss.' She turned back to Keith. 'We got it to do the van but it was too bright. Good for a shop, though. Excuse me asking, but what are those lines on your face?'

For a moment Keith didn't know what she was talking about. Then he realized.

'It was the sheet,' he explained. 'When I was asleep last night. It got scrunched up under my face.'

He didn't explain that it had been a dust sheet. Or that it had got scrunched up because he'd been tense all night in case Curly had come by and found him sleeping on the store verandah and called the cops.

The woman's husband appeared with a four litre

paint can and the woman insisted on opening his mouth and showing Keith the filling. Keith didn't mind because the can was two-thirds full.

The next four vans didn't have any paint, but then Keith hit the jackpot.

A youngish bloke with tattoos stuck his head out of his caravan window and grinned when he heard what Keith was doing.

'Your lucky day, mate,' he said.

He told Keith how he'd been employed by the Department of Main Roads to paint the white posts by the side of the highway and how he'd painted them all the way to the opal fields and then had got bored and chucked it in.

'Do you need any brushes or turps?' he asked as he pulled the tarpaulin off the back of his van.

'No thanks,' said Keith, wishing he hadn't spent all his money except eleven cents buying brushes and turps from Curly.

The bloke swung a ten litre drum off the back of the van.

'It's white,' he said, 'with reflective particles.'

Keith couldn't believe his luck.

He thanked the bloke and said he hoped the bloke found enough opals to pay someone else to paint the white posts. Then he started rolling the drum towards the store.

After a bit he stopped.

A news bulletin was just beginning on a radio in one of the vans.

Keith listened carefully, but there was no mention of any nationwide searches.

Keith wondered why not.

Perhaps Mum and Dad hadn't gone to the police.

Perhaps they didn't want to find him.

Perhaps they were glad he'd gone.

He pushed the thoughts out of his mind.

He was much too busy to be a worry wart.

By the time Keith was halfway round the diggings, word had spread that he was doing up Curly's place and people gave him paint without even being asked.

Two kids from the Aboriginal family Keith had met the day before ran up and gave him a half tin of Royal Purple and a full tin of Mandarin Orange, which, they explained, were unwanted Christmas presents.

The ultraviolet man popped out of his corrugated iron hut and handed over a quarter litre of matt black left over from painting the metal detector he'd been using before he got his ultraviolet machine.

A man with a beard and a European accent rode up on a motor bike and tossed Keith nearly two litres of Signal Red. He said he'd been using it to paint signs around his shaft saying *Tresspassers Will Be Stabbed* but he didn't need it now because he'd become a Jehovah's Witness.

Even as Keith was thanking the man for the paint and the pamphlets, he saw the sun glinting off yet more tins as people carried them towards him across the mullock heaps.

*

Keith crouched in front of the store, picked up Dad's hammer and levered the lids off the twenty-seven tins of paint and gave them all a good stir except the four that had gone solid.

By his calculation he had eighteen and a half litres.

It'll be enough, he told himself. When Curly said twenty he probably thought I'd be slapping it on like an amateur. He didn't know I already had a fish and chip shop and a Toyota Corolla under my belt.

Keith poured the Royal Purple into the Department of Main Roads Reflective White and stirred until he had a pastel violet that was just like the Autumn Crocus on the golf buggies at the Orchid Cove Resort.

He looked at his watch.

Nine forty-three.

The woman in the pub had said that Curly usually got back from his card game on Sundays at about six.

Eight hours and seventeen minutes left.

Time to start painting.

Keith didn't look at his watch.

His neck and back and arms were aching too much to make the effort, plus there was no point as his watch was covered with a big dollop of Mongolian Beige.

He needed all his strength to keep painting and not fall off the step-ladder.

He finished the Celery Green section of the guttering and grinned wearily as the applause broke out again.

It had been like this for a couple of hours now. Every time he used up a colour the crowd that had gathered to watch would give him a clap.

That's probably what's kept me going, he thought, as he forced his wobbly legs down the step-ladder. That and the food and drink. If he'd eaten everything they'd offered him he'd have exploded and Curly's store would have been even more multicoloured than it was now.

Three verandah posts to go and he was finished.

Keith washed the brush in turps and dipped it into the Poinsettia Masonry Acrylic.

He heard a truck pull up and turned anxiously, hoping it wasn't Curly.

It was the young bloke with tattoos.

'Do you want a hand?' he yelled.

'Rack off Gibbo,' said someone in the crowd. 'This is art.'

Keith grinned again.

It wasn't just mates who knew how to say the right thing.

Then, after Keith had finished the verandah posts and was giving the door another coat to use up the Flaming Pink, he heard another truck pull up, this time with a long skid and a crunch as it ran into a parked truck.

Keith watched Curly climb out of the van.

Curly looked dazed.

Not by the accident, by what he was seeing.

Keith watched as Curly took in the Mongolian Beige roof, the Aquamarine, Morning Mist, Velvet Moss and Celery Green guttering, the Matt Black down-pipes, the Autumn Crocus walls, the Vivid Coral window frames (that was inspired although I say it myself, thought Keith, mixing the Signal Red and Mandarin Orange like that), the Flaming Pink door with the Dull Red Anti-Rust handle, and the Corfu Blue, Autumn Yellow, Pale Eggplant, Grecian Dusk and Poinsettia verandah posts.

Keith held his breath.

Curly's mouth hung open.

Then the crowd broke into cheers and applause and slapped Curly on the back and told him he had the only general store in Central Queensland that was not only a major tourist attraction but could also be used by aircraft for navigating in heavy fog.

Bit by bit Curly's face relaxed into a grin and soon he was inviting everyone in for cold drinks on the house.

On the way in he shook Keith's hand and asked Keith to autograph the bottom of the wall.

Keith proudly painted his signature with the last of the matt black and said he'd be in for a drink in a sec but first he had to do a bit of guttering he'd missed.

He forced his rubbery legs back up the step-ladder.

As he smoothed on the last brushfuls of Morning Mist he looked across the roof at the vast plain that stretched away to the horizon.

Suddenly the inside of his chest felt vast as well.

With happiness.

And the feeling didn't go away when he realized he was having it. It stayed there right up to the moment when he finished off the piece of guttering and was just about to climb down the step-ladder and saw, in the distance, coming towards him along the dirt road, getting bigger by the second, the Tropical Parrot Corolla with the Hot Sunflower speed stripes.

ELEVEN

I'm a worry wart, thought Keith.

I must be.

I'm standing here with a knot in my guts when all that's going to happen is that Mum and Dad are going to pull up in the car and jump out and fling their arms round me and laugh and cry and when they start getting cross about me running away from home I'll tell them about our exclusive use of Curly's mine for the next twenty-four hours with legal ownership of all the opals we find and they'll be so excited and overjoyed they'll do cartwheels and handstands and agree that me running away from home was the best thing that ever happened to us as a family.

The knot in his guts was still there.

He watched the Corolla skid to a stop.

His mouth was as dry as the dust swirling around him.

The doors of the Corolla flew open and Mum and Dad leapt out.

Keith's blood felt as though it was pumping around his body twice as fast as it usually did.

Maybe I'm not a worry wart, he thought hopefully, maybe I'm just excitable.

Mum and Dad were running towards him laughing and crying at the same time.

Keith decided to tell them about the mine straight away, just to be on the safe side.

'Mum,' he said, 'Dad . . .'

That was as far as he got because Mum and Dad swept him off his feet like two cyclones and hugged him and kissed him and gripped his head in their hands and buried their faces in his chest.

'Great news . . .' he said, but his voice was muffled by Mum's hair.

'. . . we've got . . .' he said, but the words were lost in Dad's armpit.

'. . . an opal mine,' he said, but neither of them could hear him because they were both talking at once.

'We thought you'd been kidnapped,' said Mum.

'We thought you'd got sick and collapsed on the way to school,' said Dad.

'We almost called the police,' said Mum.

'We almost called an ambulance,' said Dad.

'Then Tracy told us what had happened,' said Mum.

'Then Tracy told us where you'd gone,' said Dad.

Through the tangle of arms around him Keith saw something that made him stop trying to speak for several seconds.

Tracy, stepping out of the Corolla.

She gave him a nervous grin.

Then Keith realized Mum and Dad had stopped speaking too.

The lull before the storm, as Mr Gerlach always put

it when he stared quietly out the window for a few seconds before giving a noisy kid's ear a twist.

'Mum, Dad,' said Keith, 'before you get angry about me nicking off, I've got something to tell you.'

Mum and Dad gave each other a little glance.

'Son,' said Dad, his voice sounding a bit strange, 'we're not angry. We're just thankful you're OK.'

'We understand the stress you've been under, love,' said Mum.

She and Dad exchanged another glance.

At least they're not still avoiding looking at each other, thought Keith.

Then Mum and Dad noticed the store.

After they'd stared at it for a while and turned to Keith and seen the paint on his hands and clothes, their faces took on the expressions he knew so well.

Mum furrowed.

Dad drooped.

'Oh Keith,' said Mum.

'Why do you keep on doing this sort of thing?' said Dad.

'Because,' said Keith, 'I like it.'

He hadn't meant to say that.

Quickly he added what he had meant to say.

'I did it to get us an opal mine.'

He waited for Mum and Dad's delighted response.

It didn't come.

Give them time, thought Keith, they've had a long trip.

*

85

He gave them two hours.

During that time they spoke with the woman in the fluffy dressing-gown, moved into the caravan park's one overnight van, found a phone box, rang Tracy's parents, had showers, had something to eat, and asked Keith questions about his trip.

Keith kept his answers short.

Then Tracy told Keith about their trip. How the car had broken down and they'd had to wait seven hours for a man in dirty orange overalls to come and give them a tow back to his garage where he'd taken another four hours to fix the engine and had tried to sell them a microwave.

'That's Mick,' said Keith. 'I painted his mate Col's truck.'

Mum and Dad looked pained.

Tracy leaned over to Keith and whispered, 'The store looks great'.

He gave her a grateful grin.

But something was wrong.

Why did she look so anxious?

'Have you found any opal yet?' asked Tracy.

Keith decided everyone had had enough time to recover from the trip.

'That opal mine I mentioned before,' he said, 'it's ours for a whole day. We can dig up as many opals as we like and keep them.'

He waited for Mum and Dad to be overjoyed.

Mum and Dad exchanged a glance.

Mum put a hand on Dad's arm.

Silly me, thought Keith. Of course. They've had the

whole trip down here to get used to the fact that we're going to be fabulously wealthy and immensely happy.

Keith saw them swap another glance.

Look at the difference it's made to them, he thought.

Gazing into each other's eyes.

Touching each other.

'Keith,' said Dad, 'we're all going back to Orchid Cove first thing in the morning. You as well.'

Keith was sure he hadn't heard that right.

Maybe someone had just exploded some gelignite out on the diggings and the shock waves had distorted Dad's words.

Dad said it again.

Keith stared at him in disbelief.

Squinting at the road across a Tropical Parrot car bonnet for two days must have left Dad with temporary brain damage.

'Don't you understand,' Keith said to him, 'we've got our own opal mine. For a whole day. We'll never have money problems again. No more migraines or tummy upsets or arguments.'

Keith turned to Mum.

She'd understand.

'Keith,' she said, 'let's all go for a little walk and get some fresh air.'

Good idea, thought Keith. Fresh air'll help certain people's brains work properly.

They all stood up.

'Tracy,' said Mum, 'would you mind doing the washing-up while we have a little chat with Keith?'

Keith was about to protest. How dare they treat

Tracy, the person who'd helped them get to the brink of wealth and happiness, like a servant?

But before he could say anything Tracy said, 'Sure, no problem,' glancing anxiously at Mum and Dad.

Right, thought Keith angrily, wait till I get you two outside.

Outside it was dark.

They walked to the edge of the caravan park and stood staring at the mullock heaps, which were glowing faintly in the moonlight and looked to Keith like coconut macaroons.

Concentrate, Keith said to himself.

He knew it was very important to choose the right words, the words that would persuade Mum and Dad to stay for just one day so they could find the opals that would make them all happy for the rest of their lives.

But it was hard with Mum on one side and Dad on the other and both of them with an arm round his shoulders.

He didn't want to think, he just wanted to enjoy.

He decided to use telepathy and sent a double-strength message to both of them.

Change your minds.

'Keith,' said Dad softly, 'I wasn't being honest with you before.'

It's working, thought Keith joyfully.

'I wasn't either,' said Mum, 'we both weren't.'

'That's OK,' said Keith, 'I understand.'

'Keith,' said Mum, and there was a little sob in her voice which made Keith realize with a stab of fear that he didn't understand at all.

'Love,' she went on, 'Dad and I have decided to split up.'

'Not just in the shop,' said Dad, the sob in his voice too. 'For good.'

'But we want you to know,' said Mum, 'that we both love you as much now as we always have.'

'And we always will,' said Dad.

Keith knew what he should be saying.

That it would only take a day.

Half a day.

A couple of hours.

And that once they had the opals they could all stay together for ever.

But he couldn't get the words out through the numbness.

All he could do was stare at the mullock heaps, which were still glowing faintly in the moonlight and looked to Keith like graves.

TWELVE

Later, after Mum had whispered to Dad that Keith probably wanted to be by himself for a bit and they'd both hugged him and gone back to the caravan, Keith saw a torch beam moving towards him through the darkness.

For a moment Keith thought it was Mum come back to tell him they'd changed their minds.

It was Tracy.

'You OK?' she asked as she got nearer.

Keith turned and stared at the mullock heaps.

He'd never felt less OK in his life.

'Have they decided to do it?' Tracy asked softly. 'They were yakking on about it for hours in the car when they thought I was asleep. Are they gunna split up?'

Keith bit his lower lip hard so the pain was all he'd have to think about.

It didn't work.

He turned and glared at Tracy.

'One more day, that's all I needed,' he said bitterly. 'If you hadn't stuck your mug in I'd have been OK.'

In the glow from the torch he could see how much he'd hurt her.

Tough.

He didn't have time to worry about that.

He stared up at the black sky.

The stars glittered like a school bag full of opals emptied out on to a bank manager's desk.

It wasn't too late.

He turned and ran into the darkness.

The pickaxe he'd spotted while he was painting the store was still there, lying half under the verandah.

Keith grabbed it and hurried out into the diggings.

It wasn't easy moving fast. The rough ground was strewn with loose rocks and pitted with tyre tracks and fossickers' trenches.

He stumbled and if it hadn't been for Tracy hurrying behind him with the torch he'd have fallen down a shaft. She helped him up.

Which is the least she can do, thought Keith bitterly, after the damage she's done.

Then he saw it.

Keep Out.

Curly's mine.

He turned to Tracy, put his finger to his lips, crept up to the old caravan and listened.

Nothing.

He dropped the pickaxe into the dark shaft and uncoiled the wire from the winch. Tracy shone the torch on him while he slithered down, then threw it down to him.

He turned towards the tunnel.

'What about me?' hissed Tracy down the shaft.

Keith gave a long-suffering sigh and shone the torch up on her while she came down.

He had to admit, even though he didn't want to, that she was a good climber.

They went along the tunnel, the torch beam making the coloured bands of rock stand out like veins. The rusty metal poles holding the roof up threw eerie crisscross patterns ahead of them.

Keith stopped and peered at a patch of rock.

He was sure he'd seen it glitter.

'If there was opal here,' said Tracy, 'they wouldn't have continued the tunnel on.'

That's just what he'd been thinking. Even though she didn't deserve it, he had to admit she was pretty smart.

Eventually they came to the end of the tunnel. The roof had gradually got lower and now they both had to crouch.

This is it, thought Keith, as he ran his hand over the different layers of rock.

They're in here somewhere.

He wished he'd asked Curly if the opals were in the smooth, hard rock or the rough, crumbly stuff.

Oh well, he'd soon find out.

He handed the torch to Tracy and gripped the pickaxe in both hands. Then he swung it as hard as he could. The metal point smashed into a layer of hard rock. Pain shot up Keith's arms and made his head ring.

He aimed the next swing at a crumbly layer. A shower of fragments sprayed over him but the pain in his arms was only half as bad.

He decided to concentrate on the crumbly layer.

*

Keith kept swinging until he couldn't feel the pick handle in his hands any more.

Then he stopped, gasping for breath, and looked closely at the rock wall. Nothing shimmered in the torchlight. No flashes of colour. No opals. Yet.

He flexed his shoulders to try to get rid of the ache, and got ready to swing the pickaxe again.

'Shall I have a go?' asked Tracy.

Keith opened his mouth to say yes, but that's not what came out.

'This isn't a tourist attraction,' he heard himself saying.

Half of him felt bad he was saying it and half of him felt good.

'That's why you're here, isn't it,' he went on, 'cause you want to travel and see the world, starting with a tour of the opal fields and a bit of opal mining?'

Tracy stared at him.

She looked even more hurt than before.

Then suddenly her eyes flashed angrily in the torchlight.

'The reason I'm here,' she said, 'is because after you nicked off your mum and dad were in such a hysterical mess they weren't thinking straight. They were gunna try and get here inland from Orchid Cove, down the stock route. People have died trying to drive down there in Corollas.'

Keith had a sudden vision of Mum and Dad sitting in their broken down car on the stock route, hungry lizards circling closer and closer.

'My dad was off working and my mum had Mrs

Newman's daughter Gail's kids,' Tracy was saying, 'so I was the only one around to navigate. It's not easy, navigating for someone who gets the trots as often as your old man. We spent half our time looking for thick scrub.'

Keith almost grinned, until he remembered that wasn't what he was meant to be feeling.

'You still didn't have to blab about what I was doing in the first place,' he said.

Tracy's shoulders slumped.

'I didn't want to,' she said, 'but when your mum and dad found you weren't at my place they went hysterical. They were gunna call the cops. There'd have been a nationwide search. Helicopters. Tracker dogs. TV. Reporters. You could have been shot or chewed up or featured on TV while you were crying or something.'

Keith looked at the concerned frown creasing her freckled forehead and suddenly he felt like swinging the pickaxe at his own bum.

How could he have been so scungy to the best mate he'd ever had?

'Sorry I've been carrying on like a wally,' he said.

'You mean a prawn,' she grinned.

'Yeah,' he said.

He told her he'd have another bash with the pickaxe, then she could have a go.

His second swing dislodged a rock the size of the big opal in Curly's store. He broke it in half with the pick, but it was just rock all the way through.

'Keith,' said Tracy softly, 'do you think this is gunna work?'

'It's got to,' he said, ''cause we haven't got any dynamite and Curly keeps his rock drill under the tinned fish.'

'No,' said Tracy, 'I mean even when we strike opal. Do you think the money's gunna make your mum and dad want to stay together?'

It's the fatigue, thought Keith, as he swung the pick-axe into the rock wall. She's been on the road for two days with Mum and Dad arguing all the time. No wonder she's over-tired and being a worry wart.

'My Auntie Fran and Uncle Leo split up,' said Tracy, 'and they were loaded. From Uncle Leo's mega insurance payout when he fell into the combine harvester.'

Don't listen to her, Keith told himself, or she'll have you being a worry wart too.

He moved his feet further apart and swung the pick-axe back as far as he could and smashed it into the rock.

Still no opals.

He swung it back again.

It hit something with a loud clang.

Tracy screamed.

Keith turned, and saw that the rusty iron roof support behind him was buckling in the middle. A gash of raw new metal was opening up as the support bent more and more out of shape.

Keith flung himself at it and tried to push it straight again.

Dust and small rocks showered onto him from the tunnel roof.

'Run,' he yelled at Tracy.

He could feel tremors and shudders running through the rock above his head. He pushed at the support with all his strength but even as he did he could feel that the force pressing down from above was a million times stronger than him.

The metal bent under his hands like a soggy chip and the last thing he saw, after Tracy had disappeared in a cloud of dust and falling rock, was a brief vision of Mum and Dad standing up on the surface, their weight added to the mass that was crushing him.

THIRTEEN

It was black with flashing colours.

Good grief, thought Keith, I'm looking at the biggest opal in the world.

Then he realized his eyes were closed.

He opened them.

Everything looked just as black, but without the colours.

He blinked a few times.

Still black.

For a moment he thought he was having the dream he'd once had where Elvis Presley crept into his bedroom and tried to smother him with a giant potato scallop.

But that couldn't be right because nobody was singing 'Are You Lonesome Tonight?'

Then he remembered where he was.

Lying in a mine with sharp rocks sticking into his back.

Perhaps they were opals.

He didn't give a stuff, they were still sharp.

He experimented with moving his arms and legs.

They all moved.

Several of them hurt, but not in a major way, not like when he'd fallen off his bike when he was seven and had ended up with eleven stitches in his leg and forty-seven in his trousers.

He groped around for any big rocks that might be lying on his chest which he hadn't felt yet on account of shock and having two T-shirts on.

There weren't any.

He sat up.

Colours exploded in front of his eyes as his head came into contact with something hard which felt like Col's truck reversing into him but which, Keith decided as he lay back down, was just a rock.

Best not to move.

Any number of giant slabs could be balanced on each other, just waiting for a nudge to come crashing down on him.

Then he remembered Tracy.

'Tracy!' he shouted.

He held his breath and listened.

Nothing.

Just the pounding of the veins in his head.

He remembered the last moment he'd seen her, standing as the dust came down, torn between getting away and staying to help.

He seemed to remember that she'd started to run.

Towards him.

Then nothing.

'Tracy!' he yelled.

He strained to hear a reply.

Even one muffled by tonnes of fallen rocks and opals.

Nothing.

He tried again.

He kept on trying till his voice was cracked and sobbing.

Then he stopped because he knew it was useless.

She couldn't hear him.

A long time later, when he'd finished crying, he hoped she hadn't felt any pain.

They'd talked about dying once, on the jetty near the fish co-op. Tracy had told him her approach was to stay cheerful because any day could be your last, specially if it was a day when the tuck shop had Mrs Reece's curry turnovers.

Keith wondered if he'd be able to stay cheerful now, trapped down here.

He wondered if he'd feel any pain, apart from the rocks sticking into his back.

He wondered how long it took twelve-year-old boys who were normally pretty healthy but who'd been under a lot of stress lately to starve to death.

Then he made himself stop wondering.

Six months ago, on a drizzly street in South London, he'd decided he wasn't going to spend the rest of his life being a misery guts and a worry wart.

Think positive.

When I get out of this, Keith thought, I'm going to put a brass plate on Curly's store dedicating the paint job to Tracy. And I'm going to write to Col and get him to put one on his truck painting.

Then he had an even better idea.

He'd do a special painting, just for Tracy. A huge painting, on hundreds of pieces of plywood stuck together, of her in all the places in the world she'd wanted to visit.

Tracy admiring the view at a campsite in Alaska. Tracy waterskiing in Venice. Tracy climbing a mountain range in Egypt. Tracy checking out all the flat but interesting places in Peru. Tracy visiting all the traditional villages in remote valleys untouched by the modern world around Melbourne.

It would be the most fabulous painting anyone had ever painted.

Keith lay there in the dark and he could see every detail, even though his eyes had filled with tears again.

Because she'd still be dead.

A painting wouldn't bring her back.

He couldn't bring her back any more than he could make Mum and Dad fall in love again.

He let the hot tears run down his cheeks even though he knew he'd regret it later when he was suffering from dehydration.

After a while he knew something else.

If it'd bring Tracy back to life, he'd help Mum and Dad pack their bags so they could split up tomorrow.

Even if it meant Dad going to live in an Alaskan campsite and only seeing him every other weekend when the ice had thawed.

Or Mum going to live up an Egyptian mountain and only seeing her every other weekend when the camels were running.

Suddenly Keith heard himself shouting it, screaming it at the top of his voice, so they'd know.

'Split up!'

'Split up!'

'Split up!'

He kept on shouting it until his throat was raw and
he'd run out of tears.

And until something had happened that made him
suddenly go silent and strain every muscle in his body
to hear better.

A familiar voice, faint and grumpy, coming from
somewhere close.

'Keep the noise down, you dopey mongrel.'

FOURTEEN

Keith sat up and banged his head again.

He didn't care.

'Tracy,' he screamed, hoarse with delight as well as all the shouting he'd just done.

'I'm over here,' she mumbled. 'Put a sock in it, I've got a headache.'

Keith felt himself go weak with relief. Before he could move towards her voice, a blinding light smacked him in the eyes.

It was so bright that at first Keith thought it was a rescue light attached to a giant drill that had drilled through the rock to them without him noticing because he'd been so busy yelling.

But when he peeped through his fingers he saw it was just the torch.

Holding it, sprawled on the ground nearby, one hand over her eyes, was Tracy.

'Are you OK?' he croaked.

She was covered in dust, and the rip in the knee of her jeans that she'd been carefully cultivating was about three times as long as it had been, and she had a big bruise over one eye.

'I think I was knocked out,' said Tracy. 'In fact I'm sure I was 'cause it happened to me once in softball and I dreamed about Peru that time as well. What about you?'

'I wasn't too good a minute ago,' said Keith, 'but now I'm great.'

They compared bruises and Keith told her he'd thought she'd been killed and she said it'd take more than a softball bat or sixty thousand tonnes of rock to do that.

She told him she'd thought he'd been a goner too for about four seconds until he'd started making more noise than Ryan Garner's brother's garage band.

They grinned and hugged each other.

Then they realized what they were doing and both gave in to a sudden urge to study their surroundings.

It took Keith a few moments to realize that the space they were in, which was about the size of the average store room in the average fish and chip shop but with a lower ceiling, was actually the end of the tunnel.

Blocking the way out was a wall of fallen rocks.

'Let's see if we can get through,' said Tracy.

They hurled themselves at the rocks and clawed and dug with their hands until they were exhausted.

They moved three small ones.

Which allowed them to see even bigger ones behind.

This is hopeless, thought Keith. Half the tunnel could be collapsed.

He didn't say anything because he didn't want to depress Tracy.

'Half the tunnel's probably collapsed,' said Tracy.

Keith said it probably wasn't quite that bad.

'What's the time?' asked Tracy.

Keith looked at his watch.

All he could see was Mongolian Beige.

'They must have noticed we're missing by now,' he said. 'Let's try shouting in case they're up top.'

He took a deep breath.

'Help!' he yelled as loudly as he could, hoping his lungs didn't rupture with the effort. 'Help!'

Tracy put her hand on his arm and told him how her Uncle Wal had told her that people always took more notice if you shouted Fire.

'Fire!' they yelled. 'Fire!'

Then Tracy remembered that Aunty Cath had pointed out that in their neck of the woods there was one word that always turned people's heads more than Fire.

'Rain!' shouted Tracy. 'Rain!'

Keith joined in and they shouted it till he thought his throat was bleeding.

Then they listened.

Nothing.

'They can't hear us,' croaked Keith. 'Must be cause they're making so much racket up top getting all the rescue equipment into position.'

Tracy agreed that must be the reason.

They sat and stared at the pattern the torch beam made on the wall of fallen rocks. On the ground Keith noticed a flat piece of metal about as big as a pizza box that had been wedged between the top of the support and the roof of the tunnel.

He caught himself wondering if he'd ever have another pizza.

Think positive.

He wished he felt as confident about the rescue equipment as he'd sounded.

Think positive.

He glanced at Tracy.

Good old Tracy, he said to himself, she hasn't had a negative thought in her whole life.

'If they don't find us,' said Tracy quietly, 'in two hundred years we'll be dust and nobody'll ever know we were here.'

Keith stared at her, shocked.

What we need, he thought, is something to take our minds off things.

Then he had an idea.

'Do you remember what Mr Gerlach said once, about what people do when they want to live for ever? They have their portraits painted.'

Now it was Tracy's turn to stare at him.

Keith picked up the piece of metal and dusted it off.

'This'll do for a canvas,' he said, 'now all I need is some paint.'

He remembered they were down a mine.

I'm going stupid, he thought. The oxygen down here must be running out and starving my brain.

Then he saw what Tracy was doing and decided her brain must be short of oxygen too.

She was on her knees, scooping dust into a pile.

When she'd finished she crouched by the opposite wall.

'OK,' she said, turning away and putting one hand

over her eyes and pointing to the pile of dust with the other, 'pee on it.'

'Don't move,' said Keith, 'I've only got the freckles to do.'

He dabbed on some freckles as lightly as he could.

It wasn't bad, this dust paint, even if it did pong a bit. It was very similar to the dull red anti-rust paint, only grittier.

And even though he hadn't done finger painting since he was three, the result wasn't looking too bad at all.

'Finished,' he said.

Tracy got up from where she'd been sitting holding the torch half on her and half on him, and took the piece of metal.

She held it out, shone the torch on it, and studied it seriously.

Oh no, thought Keith, she doesn't like it. I'm stuck down a mine with an angry critic.

She gave a big grin.

'Ripper,' she said. 'It's even better than the cane toad. Thanks.'

Keith glowed.

'When we get out,' he said, 'I'll frame it for you.'

'If we get out,' she said.

'OK,' said Keith quickly, 'now it's my turn.'

He took the piece of metal and turned it over. The other side was mottled with rust stains and mineral deposits that had leached out of the rock.

If he painted his face on it he really would look like a cane toad.

His shoulders slumped.

Tracy shone the torch over the ground and around the walls.

'How about that?' she said.

Keith peered into the ring of the torch beam.

Against the side wall of the tunnel was a sheet of corrugated iron about half as tall as him.

He tried to pull it away but it was fixed to the rock.

'Must be to stop subsidence,' said Keith. 'Doesn't matter, it's OK where it is.'

He crouched down, dusted it off with one of his T-shirts and got to work.

It wasn't easy, he discovered, painting yourself from memory, specially if you'd never painted yourself before even with a mirror.

It took ages, with a lot of thinking and trying to remember what he looked like in the photo on the shelf in the living room at home.

He hoped Tracy wasn't getting bored.

He could hear her behind him, scraping rocks.

'Don't hurt your hands tunnelling,' he said, 'It's a waste of time. Wait for them to come to us.'

'I'm not tunnelling,' she said, 'I'm writing.'

Keith turned and saw that she'd scratched a word onto the end wall of the tunnel with a rock.

Peru.

'Peru?' said Keith.

'It's a reminder,' she said quietly. 'For later on. When we get weak. So we don't give up too easily.'

Keith stared at it.

Then he finished his painting.

'What do you think?' he said.

Tracy looked at it thoughtfully.

'Looks better than the Corolla,' she said, and gave him a little grin. 'It's great. It's got that expression you get when you're thinking. The one that makes you look like that guy on telly.'

Keith didn't ask which guy in case she meant Bugs Bunny.

'There is just one thing, though,' she went on. 'You look about seven.'

Keith stared at the painting.

She was right.

The face, the hair, the expression in the eyes.

It was a little kid.

Why had he done that?

He thumped the corner of the corrugated iron with his fist in frustration. Dust fell away from around the edges. And suddenly Keith felt something he hadn't felt before.

A draught.

Coming from behind the sheet of iron.

He grabbed the piece of metal with Tracy's portrait on it, wedged it behind the sheet of iron, and twisted as hard as he could.

'Hey,' said Tracy, 'don't do that, it doesn't matter about you looking young, it's good. And you're scratching mine.'

Rusty screws snapped and popped out and the iron sheet tore away from the rock.

Keith and Tracy stared at what was behind it.

A tunnel.

It was narrow but it was big enough to crawl along.

'Come on,' said Keith.

He went first with the torch.

The rock floor of the tunnel was murder on their knees, but it didn't matter because after they went round a curve they could see grey light up ahead.

A few minutes later they crawled out into the bottom of a shaft.

A wire ladder with bits of plastic pipe for rungs hung down from the top. They flung themselves up it without stopping for breath and suddenly they were out in the open air, lying on a mullock heap, gasping and laughing, the sky above them streaked with dawn light.

Keith heard a generator chug into life over on the next heap and looked across and saw a crowd of people standing around the shaft to Curly's mine. They were silhouetted against the rising sun, but he could make out Mum and Dad.

'Let's go and surprise them,' he said, getting up.

'Wait,' said Tracy. 'I've got something to show you.'

Keith saw that she was clutching the piece of metal with her portrait on it to her chest.

Even as he was trying to find a way of telling her how good that made him feel without sounding mushy, Tracy put her hand into her pocket and pulled out a dirty rock the size of a medium flathead fillet, battered.

'It's the one I was writing with,' she said. 'Didn't know what it was till the end broke off.'

As she held it out to him, the first weak rays of the

sun hit it and colours flashed out of it just like they had out of the opal in Curly's store.

Except, thought Keith as he gazed at it, the colours in Curly's opal were watercolours and these are oils.

Cobalt, vermilion, magenta, that sort of stuff.

He looked at Tracy holding the painting and the opal, and suddenly he knew what he had to do.

He grabbed the torch and ran to the shaft and started climbing down the ladder.

'No!' shouted Tracy, 'Don't be a dill! Come back!'

The tunnel was as hard on his knees as it had been before, and when Keith staggered back into the cavity they'd just escaped from he heard the roar of drills and saw that the roof was trembling and dust was falling all around him.

He didn't care.

There, on the ground in front of him, was what he'd come for.

As he picked it up, the torchlight and the tears in his eyes made it flash momentarily with a million points of coloured light.

Even at that instant, when it looked like a dazzling sheet of opal instead of a piece of corrugated iron, he could still see, clearly, himself.

FIFTEEN

From the moment Keith climbed out of the shaft, it was chaos.

There were faces all around him, and lights, and voices all speaking at once.

Mum and Dad were hugging him and crying all over him.

He tried to tell them to be careful of his painting because corrugated iron rusted easily, but they weren't listening.

He saw the Corolla parked nearby, headlights aimed at the shaft, so he went and put the painting in the boot.

Then two men in white overalls led him over to a bright yellow tent sitting next to a red helicopter.

Tracy came out of the tent and saw him and broke into a huge relieved grin.

'Jeez you're a prawn,' she said and hugged him so tight Keith could feel his face going as red as the helicopter, partly from embarrassment and partly because she was squeezing all his blood up into his head.

He was glad when he got into the tent and discovered that the two men in overalls were doctors. At least doctors were used to that sort of physical contact.

While the doctors checked him over they explained they were from a nearby coal mine, only four hundred kilometres away, and that they often came over to patch people up and do a bit of fossicking.

Then he found himself back outside with a blanket round his shoulders and hot drink in his hands and all sorts of people he'd seen on the diggings crowding round him.

The ultraviolet man touched his blanket for luck.

A middle-aged woman in a cardigan and gumboots who Keith didn't recognize until he saw that she was wearing a fluffy dressing-gown underneath, took his photo.

The ex-Department of Main Roads post painter offered him a beer until the woman in the fluffy dressing-gown told him to stop it.

Then Curly, bald head and wrinkled face looking strangely off-white even in the yellow rays of the morning sun, gripped his arm and took him to one side.

'Sorry I damaged your mine,' said Keith.

'Don't worry about that,' said Curly, 'and anything you found is yours, no questions.'

He leant closer with an anxious glance around to make sure no one was listening and Keith could see that he was going to ask at least one question.

'That tunnel you escaped through,' muttered Curly, 'the one that runs from my claim into the, um, claim next to mine, has anyone asked you about it?'

Keith was just about to say no when they were interrupted by the roar of a motor bike. The man with the beard and the European accent got off and came over to Curly and handed him a wooden sign daubed with faded red lettering.

It said *Tresspassers Will Be Stabbed*.

Curly went even more off-white.

The man took the sign back and handed Curly some Jehovah's Witness pamphlets.

Then Mum and Dad appeared with Tracy.

Keith saw that Mum and Dad were holding hands.

'Come on love,' said Mum to Keith, 'let's all go for a little walk.'

The sun was above the horizon as they walked slowly between the mullock heaps.

Keith tried to concentrate on the warmth on his face so he'd forget the knot in his guts.

It was no good.

Every time he glanced at Mum and Dad holding hands it got tighter.

Then Tracy spoke.

'Shall I go first, Mr and Mrs Shipley?' she asked.

'All right love,' said Mum, 'you go first.'

'Keith,' said Tracy, giving him a big grin, 'this is for you.'

She held out the opal.

'I know I found it,' she went on, 'but we wouldn't be here if it wasn't for you nicking off, and we wouldn't have been down that mine if it wasn't for you painting the store, and I wouldn't have been writing stuff on the wall if it wasn't for you keeping my spirits up, so it's really yours.'

She put it into his hand.

Keith looked at it for a long time because he wanted to choose exactly the right words for what he was going to say.

He looked at Tracy and his guts tingled so much that they almost unknotted.

'Jeez you're a dopey mongrel,' he said, grinning. 'And if you don't send me a postcard from Peru I'll come over there and boot you up the bum.'

He put the opal back into her hand.

Dad cleared his throat.

'Keith,' he said, 'before you react hastily, wait till you understand why Tracy's making such a generous offer.'

He cleared his throat again.

Oh no, thought Keith, Dad's got to have his tonsils out and it's to pay for the operation.

But he knew that wasn't the real reason.

'Keith,' said Dad, 'Mum and me have talked about it for most of the night, and we've decided not to split up.'

'We've decided to stay together,' said Mum. 'For your sake. We've talked about it and we're determined to make it work.'

'And the opal is to help with the financial problems,' said Tracy.

Keith stared out across the mullock heaps, which were glowing in the morning sun and looked like mounds of gold.

He took a deep breath of cool, clear morning air.

This was the moment he'd come halfway across

117

Queensland for, halfway around the world really, an he'd never dreamt it would be like this.

But it was, and he knew exactly what he was goir to do.

He took another deep breath and even though h felt sadder than he ever had before, the knot in h guts was suddenly gone.

He turned back to Mum and Dad. They were bot smiling as hard as they could, but Mum's forehea was still furrowed and Dad's mouth was still droop

'That is what you want, isn't it love?' asked Mur in a shaky voice.

Keith looked at them both and slowly shook h head.

SIXTEEN

Keith peered across Trafalgar Square into the late morning fog.

Everything was grey. Grey buildings. Grey shops. Grey cars.

Nelson's Column was grey, looming up into the grey London sky.

Keith grinned.

What a great day.

He pulled Tracy's letter from his pocket and read it for the nineteenth time since it had arrived at Dad's place that morning.

Dear Keith,

Ripper, eh? Only another ten days and I'll be there. It's great you've got two bedrooms now cause that means I won't have to pay camping ground fees and I'll have more opal money left for checking out London.

My folks have said I might be able to stay for a seventh week! They're really rapt cause the new roof is on now and their bedroom doesn't leak any more.

I had a lend of a book on Peru. It still looks pretty interesting, but not as interesting as the London Underground. What happens if a train breaks down? Do they have toilets down there? Mrs Newman reckons underground trains make your feet swell. Can't wait.

Say g'day to your folks from me. It must be exciting, having a mum who's a Parking Inspector.

See you soon.

Love Tracy.

P.S. Mr Gerlach put your cane toad painting on the front of the school magazine.

PPS. When you said you painted your Dad's new shop fourteen colours, was that inside as well or just outside?

Keith put the letter back in his pocket and looked at his watch. It had been running a bit slow ever since he'd put it in the turps to get rid of the Mongolian Beige.

Eleven thirty-eight.

Or thereabouts.

Heaps of time.

He'd got four days to finish off painting his bedrooms before Tracy arrived. His room at Mum's place was just about finished except for the rainforest mural on the ceiling. And all he had to do to finish off his room at Dad's place was to put a second coat of Tropical Parrot on the wardrobe and add the Hot Sunflower speed stripes.

Keith climbed the steps of the National Gallery and went inside.

He walked slowly through the rooms, lingering in front of his favourite paintings.

As usual he didn't spend long looking at the one called *Giovanni Arnolfini and His Wife* because the man and woman reminded him of Mum and Dad before they cheered up.

Still, he thought, it's interesting that people married

the wrong people even five hundred and sixty years ago.

He noticed that the walls in one of the Early Italian rooms had been repainted.

Satin Finish Eggshell Enamel.

Not bad.

Keith wandered on through the gallery, smiling as he thought about bringing Tracy here.

After she'd checked out all the paintings, specially the Rembrandt *Self Portrait* which looked a bit like a cane toad, and he'd shown her the Flemish rooms, which desperately needed some Celery Green around the windows, he'd tell her his secret ambition.

That one day his work would be on these walls.

'Inside the picture frames or around them?' she'd ask with a grin.

He'd grin back and give a shrug.

Didn't matter.

He was a painter, not a worry wart.

Morris Gleitzman
Puppy Fat

'What section do you want to advertise in? Toys? Sporting Equipment? Computers and Video Games?' The woman in the newspaper office took off her glasses and polished them on her cardigan. 'What are you advertising?'

'My parents,' said Keith.

Keith's worried. Can two single parents with saggy tummies, wobbly bottoms and dodgy legs ever find happiness? Not a chance, decides Keith, unless he can get them into shape. Just as well Tracy the mountaineer and Aunty Bev the beautician are arriving from Australia . . .

The brilliantly funny sequel to *Misery Guts* and *Worry Warts*.

A selected list of titles available from Macmillan and Pan Books

The prices shown below are correct at the time of going to press. However, Macmillan Publishers reserve the right to show new retail prices on covers which may differ from those previously advertised.

MORRIS GLEITZMAN

Misery Guts	0 330 32440 3	£3.50
Worry Warts	0 330 32845 X	£3.50
Puppy Fat	0 330 34211 8	£3.50
Blabber Mouth	0 330 33283 X	£3.50
Sticky Beak	0 330 33681 9	£3.50
Belly Flop	0 333 34522 2	£3.50
Water Wings	0 330 35014 5	£3.50

All Macmillan titles can be ordered at your local bookshop or are available by post from:

Book Service by Post
PO Box 29, Douglas, Isle of Man IM99 1BQ

Credit cards accepted. For details:
Telephone: 01624 675137
Fax: 01624 670923
E-mail: bookshop@enterprise.net

Free postage and packing in the UK.
Overseas customers: add £1 per book (paperback)
and £3 per book (hardback)